PAPER ROUT3

PAPER ROUT3

Di'Maryea McGhee

Library of Congress Control Number:		2021904596
ISBN:	Hardcover	978-1-6641-6197-9
	Softcover	978-1-6641-6196-2
	eBook	978-1-6641-6195-5

This is a work of fiction. Names, characters, places and incidents either are the product of the author's imagination or are used fictitiously, and any resemblance to any actual persons, living or dead, events, or locales is entirely coincidental.

Print information available on the last page.

Rev. date: 03/04/2021

To order additional copies of this book, contact:
Xlibris
844-714-8691
www.Xlibris.com
Orders@Xlibris.com
818316

Makin' Money Moves

"Man, bra, I'm tired of being broke," Young Money blurted out loud to no one in particular. Money was on the phone and texted one of his li'l freaks. It was Friday, and he was tryna be knee-deep in some pussy. Damn!

"Jay, pass the fucking blunt, nigga. You over there giving the blunt a blow job," Money had said.

"Bra, it ain't even on you," Young Money said.

"Both you niggas, sike out," Jay retorted to Young Money and Money as he passed the blunt to Money.

"Ayy, Jay, how long you said yo mom and dad gone be gone?" Money said as he inhaled the cookies he had rolled up in the back wood.

"They said they were coming back Sunday night."

Jay's parents were considered a little above middle-class; both parents had good jobs. Jay's mother worked at Kaiser Hospital as a registered nurse, and his dad worked at Tesla as an engineer. Jay's parents stayed on Oakdale in Palau. They moved from Tennessee to California when Jay was five and had found themselves a nice home. Oakdale Projects was ten feet away, damn near connected if it wasn't for some grass and a slab of cement. As for Money and Young Money, they weren't that fortunate. Money and Young Money stayed in the low-income Oakdale Housing Projects a.k.a. Oakdale Mob, considered to be a non-notorious gang that had been with several different neighborhoods throughout Hunters Point. Money and Young Money's mom was a functioning addict. She was addicted to pain medicine, anything that had an opioid in it. The dad passed before they were born, and they were told he had gotten killed by a rival gang called Big Block. That was why Money and Young Money never liked them niggas. Even though Money and Young Money weren't with that shit, all his cousins were. So one day, when Jay was outside bouncing his basketball, Money and Young Money walked up to him and said, "Give me yo basketball!"

Jay said, "No! My dad gave me this ball."

"You either give us yo ball, or I'm gonna beat yo ass."

Mind you, Money and Young Money were only like six years old around that time. So Jay said, "I guess we gonna be fighting!"

Money walked up to Jay and pushed him, and Jay pushed him back. Then they started wrestling as Young Money stood to the side and watched them break it up. "All right! That's enough. Break it up. Ayy, brah, what's yo name?" Young Money said as he was picking Jay off the ground.

"My name is Jay," Jay said as Money got off the ground, dusting himself off. He asked Young Money why he didn't help him!

"Because you always tryna punk somebody."

"I'm tellin' Moma you didn't help me."

"Yea! Whatever. Ayy, Jay, you want to go to the courts and play some ball?"

"Sure! Why not? Let me go ask my mom and dad."

Ever since then, Money and Young Money had been thick as thieves, literally ever since.

"Jay! Earth to Jay," Young Money said. "Are you ever gon' pass the blunt? You over there in La La Land."

Jay had chuckled as he passed the blunt to Young Money. "Nah, bruh, I was just thinking 'bout that time when we first met."

"Ayy, that was some mean shit," Money said, giving off a fake laugh.

"Wassup, Jay? Let's slide to WingStop," Young Money said.

Jay was the only one who had a car courtesy of his parents for completing high school and graduating on time. Now it was summer! And they had nothing but free time on their hands.

"As long as it ain't the one by Martin Luther King Park," Money said.

"Nah, we gonna go to the one in Daly City. It be hella li'l bitches at that one. Make sure you order the food first," Money told Young Money.

"Nigga, what, I look like yo bitch? Aaah, shit here we go again. Both you niggas sound like some bitches."

Jay grabbed his phone off the charger and dialed WingStop. Ring! Ring! "Hello, WingStop, how may I help you?"

"Yeah, can I get a twenty-piece lemon pepper chicken with fries? And a Sprite. What y'all getting?"

"Get me, awe damn, what I want? Oh! I know what I want. Get me tha five pieces, hot wings, three pieces of lemon pepper, five parmesan, and five barbeque, and a cherry Sprite," said Young Money.

"Ayy, Money, what you want?"

"Get me the same thing YM got."

Jay shook his head. "Both you niggas is weirdos. How long is the wait?"

"It should be around thirty minutes, okay!"

"Thank you."

"As nice as nigga," Young Money said to Jay.

"It's called having manners," Jay said.

"Yea, whatever, nigga."

Ayy, Money, you been text'n that same-ass bitch. Wassup with them hoes? They gonna pull up or what?" Jay had said.

"I'm tryna see right now. Ayy, the food should be done right about now. Let's go get that shit."

As Jay, Money, and Young Money pulled up, they saw a clean-ass CK 500 Benz in the parking lot.

"I wonder who that car is," Young Money had said to himself.

"Pick up order for James Bond!"

Young Money walked up to the register. As he was walking to the register, he spotted a badass Asian bitch to his left, sitting down eating with her friends, and it tripped Young Money out, that her friends were black. They all had on scrubs, so he knew they were some kind of nurses. Young Money walked back over to where his brother and Jay were sitting and handed them their food. He told them to hold on right quick and walked off. He did the breath check to make sure his shit wasn't kickin' and checked his attire. He had on a gray Champ sweat suit with some gray phone posits. As he pushed up, he greeted the group. "What's pop'n?" Like he was Cam'ron from *Paid in Full.*

"Excuse you!" one of the beautiful ladys said. "That is not how you talk to no ladies."

Young Money had said to himself, "These ole boogie-ass bitches. My bad! How you ladies doing?"

"There you go," one of the women said. "We're fine.

"Well, I really came over here to talk to yo potna," Young Money said.

"Who, Mulan?" the other girl said whose name happened to be Talor.

"Young Money introduced himself. "What's good? My name Young Money."

"Boy, yo momma didn't name you no Young Money," Keyanna had said.

"Little do you know she did."

"Well, my name is Mulan. Nice to meet you."

"Nice to meet you too!" Young Money said. "I came over here because I thought you was cute, and I was wondering if I can get to know you."

"I don't know. You prolly some type of stalker or something."

"Nah! That ain't my steelo. I don't get down like that!" Young Money said.

"Nah, I'm just playing. You can get to know me. My number (510)245-3681, aight?"

"I'ma tap in," Young Money said.

As he walked off, Jay had said, "Damn, nigga, what you was telling lil baby, yo whole life story?"

"Shut up, nigga. I just nocked a bad bitch. I ain't gon' lie, she is bad," Money said on the way back to Jay's spot. Young Money was thinking 'bout the girl he just nocked. Money was sitn in the front seat fuckin' his food up, smackn' loud as fuck, eatin' like it was his last meal.

"Ayy! YM!" Money was saying in between bites. "What's poppin'! Why you was acting like GQ smooth on shit when you was getn' at ole girl?"

"You know how I do," Young Money said with a slight grin. "Once everybody got back to Jay's house," Young Money said to himself, but out loud! So everybody could hear. "Back to the basics," with a huff at the end.

"What's that supposed to mean?" Jay said.

"Nigga, it mean we do the same bullshit every weekend, get high, get some drank, eat WingStop, and call them some ass bitches that come and smoke all our weed and drink all are duce."

"Okay! Nigga you act like that's a problem. At least we gon' fuck dem bitches," Jay said.

"Young Money, you been on some weirdo shit all day, fuck! You got going on?" Money said.

"I got a lot going on. I'm tryna get paid."

"Well, get ass a job like me and Jay."

"My nigga, I ain't finna be mopn' no floors or none of that shit. I need some real money."

"Yeah! Whatever, nigga," Money said.

"Where you going, bra?"

"I'm finna go to the house real quick. I'ma holla at you niggas in a few.

Mulan was considered a bad bitch, and she knew it! Everytime she looked in the mirror, she told herself that. Mulan was 5'5" with light-brown chinky eyes, courtesy of her Asian side. She was petite, slim waisted, flat stomached, with a nice lil bubble booty, not too small and not too big, and it was soft. Mulan got her exotic looks from her mother, who was full Asian, and her dad, who was full African American. They met at Galileo High School, and everybody knew that gal was full of bing bings! And all through high school, Mulan's parents were inseparable, until after they graduated. Mulan's mom got accepted to Cal Berkeley, and her dad decided to go to the Marines. Mulan's mom found out she was four weeks pregnant. After this, he left, and she made her mind up to keep it, but she wanted to get her parents' approval. Mulan's mom's parents were strict believers of dating within their own race, so when she told her parents, they gave her an ultimatum. Get an abortion, or they would disown her. So she made the hardest decision of her life and told them she was keepin' her baby. And since day 1, it's been Mulan and her mom. Her dad got killed in the line of duty when Mulan was ten years old. And up till now, she resented her grandparents and everybody on her mom's side of the family because they looked at her as the black sheep of the family. As Mulan finished admiring herself in the closet mirror, she rubbed cocoa butter all over her petite frame. She massaged her firm pencey breast, her arm, down her stomach, her legs, and her feet. As she was doing this, she was saying to herself, "I can't believe I'm still a virgin. Yes! I can. Niggas ain't shit! All these niggas are the same dog-ass selfish, inconsiderate, people. That's why my ass still a virgin. These niggas ain't worthy. My mom taught me right, to wait on Mr. Right, but shot! A bitch is sho tired of waiting. I want to feel how my cuzn Fendi in Chamele be feeln', how they niggas be fucking them every which way and how they be telln me how they niggas be makem them cum. The only thing making me cum is Bently, my vibrator. That thing be driven me crazy, and hear am twenty years old, single and fa sho ready to fuck. But then again, I'm good because whoever I give this pussy to, he gonna be all mine, period, cause I don't believe in sharing." Ring! Ring! Ring! "Who the fuck is FaceTiming me? Who is this?"

"It's Young Money."

"Young Money? I don't know no Young Money."

"We met at the WingStop earlier," Young Money said.

"Oh yea! I remember you now. Lil rudeness."

"I ain't rude. Nah, I'm just playen. My cuzzns thought you was."

"Those were yo cuzns how them yo cuzzns and you askin'?" Young Money said.

Asian and black Mulan corrected him. "And how is that? If you must know, my mom is Asian, and my dad is black. Anything else, nosey?" Mulan said.

"So what? You some type a nurse or som'thing?" Young Money said.

"I mean, you can say that," Mulan said.

"Why you say it like that?"

"Because I'm tryna finish school to become a registered nurse, and right now between my pharmacy job at Walgreens and paying my rent and keeping up with school, that shit can be overwhelming."

"I know what you mean," Young Money said.

"But anyway," Mulan said. "How old is you?"

"I'm eighteen!" Young Money said. "What about you?"

"I'm twenty years old, but I'll be the big two-one this year. November 10th."

"Oh! So you a Scorpio," Young Money said with a smirk. "Look at you, lil nasty."

"Get yo mind out the gutter. All Scorpios aren't freaks! Unlike myself, I'ma very grounded person, very territorial! And I speak my mind straight up," Mulan said. "And when is yo birthday, if you don't mind me asking."

"My b-day fenna come up in a few more months."

"And what month is that?" Mulan asked.

"December 27th."

"So you a Capricorn, huh!" Now it was Mulan's turn to give her opinion.

"What you gotta say?" Young Money said.

"Oh! Nothing, just you Capricorns is sneaky, possessive, crazy. Shall I go on? Ayy! You siked out for real."

"Nah! I know my shit," Mulan said.

"Well, let me learn you something. Me personally, I'm none of these, but I can get a lil crazy if somebody fuck with me the wrong way."

"Let me not get on yo bad side then."

"Nah, you cool. I kinda like you," Young Money said.

"Is that right! You don't even know me," Mulan said.

"I know, but I'm tryna get to know you, and I think you cute."

"Aww, thank you! You not to bad looking yoself," Mulan stated.

"Ayy! Let me ask you something," Young Money said. "Who you fuck wit?"

"To be honest, I'm single. I don't got time for niggas. All they want is some pussy, and on to the next. What about you?" Mulan said.

"Well, let's see. I got a few friends, nothing too violent. I ain't really met no one to fuck with on that level."

"Yea! I know what you mean."

"So when I'ma get to see you again?" Young Money asked.

"I'm off the whole weeknd, so it's up to you whenever you got some free time."

"Aight, bet. We can go to Dave and Busters tomorrow, but you gon' have to come get me because my car in the shop," Young Money told her.

"It's all good! What time you tryna leave?" Mulan had asked.

"Like around seven or eight p.m.," Young Money answered.

"So this is a date?" Mulan asked.

"Yea! Something like that." Beep! Beep!

"Um, Young Money, can you call me back in, like, thirty minutes? My buggin'-ass cuzzn keep blown my phone up."

"All right, I'ma tap in with you later."

Much clicked over, and all she seen was her cuzzn Chanele twerkn on her FaceTime.

"Bitch, you need to stop!" Mulan said.

"Bitch, stop hatn'. You just mad you ain't got ass like this. You need to let somebody hit that shit ole virgin ass."

"Bitch, unlike you, I have morals, and standards. Thank you very much," Mulan said.

"I got morals and standards too. Any nigga that got that bag, he can get it. I treat these niggas like hoes," said Chanele.

"Wassup thoe? What you bitches got going on?"

"Me and Chanele finna get ready to go to the rock. That bitch Falesha nigga Tom Tom, throwing a all white party. So is you coming or nah?"

"Girrlll, you know I don't do them hoes. Everytime y'all get together, you bitches get on that drunk shit and be ready to start shit," Mulan said.

"Let me find out you on some scary shit"

"Nah! I'm on some grown shit," Coco chimed in.

"Yea! Whatever, where Fendi at?" asked Mulan.

"Dat hoe in the bathroom taking all day in the shower."

"Well, tell her to call me once she get out the shower."

So Chanele asked one more time, "Is you coming?"

"No! Bitch." Mulan kicked rocks and hung up the phone. She thought about Young Money and wondered if he was gon' call back.

The next day, Young Money woke up with a smile on his face and a hard dick. *Damn, I need some pussy. I'm fenna call one of these project bitches*, he thought to himself. He was tryna figure out which one because he was fuckin' a few of them. And the cold part about it was all them bitches knew about one another in some form or action. Ring ring ring. Ole weak-ass bitch didn't answer the phone. "I'm finna call dat bitch TaTa. She stay ready," Young Money mused out loud to no one in particular. Ring ring! "Wassup stranger?" Young Money spoke into the phone.

"Good morning to you too, Young Money, and why you ain't FaceTime me? What bitch you got over there? Don't have me fuck you up," TaTa said.

"Girl gone with that shit, wassup tho? Pull up! I'm tryna see you."

"Aww, you wanna see me?" she repeated in that childlike voice she be doing. "You tryna see me and who else?" TaTa questioned.

"Just you." *This bitch siked out*, Young Money thought. "You coming or not?"

"Yea! I'm finna walk back there right now."

Five minutes later, Young Money heard knocking at the door. "I see you wasn't doing no playing."

"I was missing you too and stuff, and plus I need some dick."

"Oh, yea!" said Young Money as he grabbed her by the ass. They walked back to his room. Once they got to his room, she slid her yoga pants off. She had on some Victoria's Secret boy shorts. While Young Money was lying on his bed, TaTa started twerking for him, and he said, "You don't know what to do with all this ass. Bring it over here and I'ma show you."

Now TaTa was a bad bitch, 5'7", slim waist, nice juicy titties, high yellow, and a phat soft-ass booty. She was what you called an undercover thot. That was why Young Money never got too close to her; he knew her get-down. As TaTa walked towards him, she was tryna look seductive and sexy as she climbed on the bed. She tried to kiss him, but Young Money turned his face. So she started to kiss and lick his neck, and the only reason Young Money let her do that was because that shit felt good. And so TaTa knew that, and she kissed and licked all the way down to his dick. Once she reached it, she just stared at it and said to herself, "Damn, this nigga got pipe." She started kissing and licking down the shaft of his dick. As she put him in her mouth, she started deep-throating him. It was something about sucking his dick that turned her on as she continued to deep-throat him. Young Money was like, "Damn, TaTa, do yo thang."

She looked up at him, smiling with his dick still in her mouth. Young Money started to finger her pussy and rub on her clit. She started to moan. "Oooh! Young Money, you gonna make me cum."

"Keep sucking dat dick," Young Money demanded of her.

"Like this? You like when I suck it like this?" She continued to deep-throat him.

Young Money started to grab TaTa's head. She knew every time he did that he was finna get ready to cum. So she speeded up and swallowed every inch of his dick. As he came, she swallowed all his seed and kept sucking. Once she felt his dick getting hard again, she got on all fours, facedown, ass up! Just how Young Money liked it. As he was finna put his dick inside her soaking wet pussy, he slapped her on her phat ass, causing her to let out a low moan. Then he penetrated her, sliding inside her wet phat pussy. He then started giving her slow long strokes. She was throwing it back and telling Young Money to beat it up, so he griped both her ass cheeks and started pounding her pussy faster and faster, putting her in a trance. "Ooow, Young Money, I love this dick. Oh my god, you dat nigga. Umm huh, keep fucking me like that. I'm 'bout to cum." As she was cumming, Young Money put his thumb in her ass, and she really started to go crazy as he continued to fuck TaTa from the back.

Young Money asked, "Who pussy is this?"

TaTa was like, "This yo pussy, ooow. I swear this yo pussy. All yours."

After hearing that, Young Money started going in even harder and busted a fat nut inside TaTa. As he was done and he was still inside her, TaTa started to wiggle both her ass cheeks. He slapped her ass and slid up out of her and headed to the bathroom to go get in the shower. As he was in the shower, TaTa lay back down and logged on Twitter and wrote. It was all about Young Money. Straight up, as Young Money got out the shower, TaTa was putting her clothes on to leave. "So when I'ma get too see you again because you be acting like you too busy for a bitch?" TaTa said.

"I'ma tap in with you later," Young Money told her.

"Yea, we gon' see, and you bet not be giving my dick to nobody. You gon' have me beat one of these bitches' asses.

"Girl gone with that wild shit," Young Money said.

As TaTa was getting ready to leave, Young Money's iPhone started to ring. "Who the fuck is that calling yo phone, Young Money?"

"How I'ma know? I'm right here with you."

"Yea, all right. Play with me if you want to."

"My nigga, I'm call you later," Young Money told her.

As he walked back to his room, he had seen that it was his twin brother, Money, so he FaceTimed him back Money answered. "Wassup? YM, tha fuck happened to you last night?"

"Ain't shit happened to me. You niggas was on some dry shit, so I got on," Young Money said. Where you at anyway?" Young Money asked his twin brother.

"At Danyale's house," Money said.

"Danyale that stay on Baldwin?" Young Money asked him.

"Yea, dumbass, Danyale," Money had told him in his slow, retarded voice.

"Ayy, bra, she cooking breakfast," Young Money told his brother Money.

"Nigga, you know she always cook for a real nigga like me everytime I come over here."

"Tell her to make some for me to a nigga hungry than a muthafucka, and I just got through fucking that bitch TaTa. You know how I do," Young Money said.

"Yea, I hear you. I'ma tell her to make you a plate," Money told Young Money.

"Aight, I'm fenna put some clothes on in the walk up there. Good thing Baldwin was only up the block."

As Young Money was walking through the projects, he ran into his older cuzzin Shota. Now Shota was a thoroughbred type, a nigga. He bust that cannon, and he was about getting that bag. His street clout spoke for itself, and he was quick to knock something down if a nigga disrespected. "Wassup, lil cuzzn," Shota had yelled out to Young Money. As Young Money walked over to where Shota was at, he peeped. He was sitting in a 2017 BMW Mb Gran Coupe with a bust-down Cuban in Rolly on.

"I see who getting money in these streets," Young Money had said to his older cuzn Shota.

"Come on, man. You know how I do, lil cuzn."

"I'm saying when you gon' let me come get some money with you,"

Young Money said. "Now you know yo man gon' kill me and you, but hop in real quick. let me holla at you what's good," Young Money said.

"Check it out. I know you see me out here riding foreign bust-down and rockn' designer, but this shit don't come easy. I'm taking penitentiary chances."

"So what is it exactly that you do?" Young Money said.

"I'ma keep it all the way a hundred wit' you, lil cuzz. I be out here hittn' houses, but I don't be on K10 reckless shit like if somebody in the spot, I don't go in there. That's home invasion. Them crackas a give you all day for that shit, so what you do is you wanna go knock on the door, knock a few times, and if nobody comes answer the door, nine times out of ten, they gone. Then it's a go. You gon' need at least two more people with you. Somebody gotta sit in the car in watch the streets. You and whoever else you decide to bring gon' be the ones who go in. You gon' need a crowbar to get in the front door, or you can use a window puncher to break the window. It's always good to go in the back. So once you get in, you only want to look for jewelry in cash. That's it. Once you grab the doe in the jewelry, tap in with dude in the car. Ask him if it's good to come out, then you go to the wip in pull off and whatever jewelry you come up with. My people gon' buy it. So you got everything locked in, I'm telln' you," Shota told Young Money.

"Yea, I got chu," Young Money answered.

"All right then, lil nigga. Get you if anything hit the fan, you don't know me," Shota said.

"Come on, my nigga. You know I'm solid."

"All right then. I'm holla at you in a few/ I'm fenna yo pull up on one of my lil' freaks," Shota said.

As Young Money got out the car, walking towards Baldwin, he was thinking about what his cuzzn was tellin' him. *Damn who the fuck I'ma get to come with me to bust this move. I know who I'ma get at: Money in Jay. Yea, that's what I'ma do.*

Knock knock knock.

"Who the fuck is that banging on my door early in the morning?" Danyale was saying out loud to no one in particular. As she opened the door, Young Money was just standing there, admiring Danyale's beauty. Now Danyale was a bad chocolate bitch. People said she favored Buffie the body and even had ass like her too. "Boy, what the fuck you starin' at?" Danyale had said.

"I mean, shit. Look what the fuck you got on. A tank top in some boy shorts. All that ass you got, it's hard not to stare," Young Money said.

"Boy, whatever."

Money said, "Yo that as a brother at the door. I can't help it if these hoes be on me." He had recited a verse from Lil Boosie.

As he was walking up the stairs, she said, "They be on a nigga. They be on nigga. They wonna take Young Money home in act a donky with him."

"Damn, nigga. Took you long enough," Money said as he was inhaling the cookies he had rolled up in the back wood.

"I know. I was holln' at that nigga Shota. He was putting me on game about some shit," Young Money said. Money looked at him with a stale face. He knew what type of shit his older cuzzn was into. "Let me hit the dro," Young Money said as he was hittin' the cookie blunt. He told Money he wanted to holla at him about something.

"Yea, we definitely gon' holla," Money had said back.

"Ayy, bruh, you remember the other day when we had went to WingStop?" Young Money had said.

"Yea, what about?" Money said with an "I don't give a cuck" look on his face. "Tell me why. I'm fenna go out on a date with that Asian bitch later. Yay yay yeah," Money said in a playful voice. "What you want? A round of aplouse?"

"Oh, hatn'-ass nigga. Fuck you," Young Money said. "Pass the blunt, my nigga. That's what you need to be doing." Young Money hit the wood one more time.

Ayy, bra, I'm fenna go back to the house. Danyale, thanks for the breakfast."

"You know it's always good, young greedy YM. You coming to the gym with me and Jay. We finna get ready to leave in a minute."

"Yea, just hit me when y'all ready to leave," Young Money said.

As he was walking down the street, he seen Dango, one of his big homies, coming out the cuts. "Wassup, big bra. What you got going on?"

"All boi, you know, thugen out here. Fill me."

"I see you with that draco on the wall right there," Young Money said.

"You already know niggas just did a drill up top. Up top was big block."

"O yea, I heard them shots last night."

"Yea, man o boy got hooked down up there so be on yo shit around here."

"Most definitely," Young Money said and headed to the house.

Coco was looking at her phone, debating whether she should call Young Money.

"I don't know why you acting stub'rn. You know you want to call him," Fendi told her.

"Bitch, ain't nobody tripn' off dat nigga," Coco had said.

"You can't lie to me. I know you. You been talking 'bout that nigga since I come over here."

"Anyway, you gon' help me do my hair," Coco said.

"Yea, I got you, but you ain't going on yo lil date till later, so I'ma fenna take me a nap. Wake me up later."

"Yea, whatever, bitch."

Ring, ring, ring.

"What you want?" Coco said once she picked up the phone to Young Money.

"What's with the hostility? I see some bod woke up on the wrong side of the bed."

"Actually, I slept very good, for your information."

"But let me ask you som'thing," Mulan told him. "What happened to you calling me back last night? You probably think I'm telling you anything. Once I got off the phone with you, I ended up fallin' to sleep."

"Yea, whatever, nigga. That's strike one." Young Money took his ear off the phone and mumbled to himself, "Who this bitch think she talking too? Yea, I hear you. So wassup, we still on for later?"

"I don't know. I'm debating on that. Is you shore you want to get to know me because I don't got time for the games."

"Ain't nobody playin' games with you."

"Yea, we gon' see," Coco said. "Anyway what you got planned for today?"

"Me, my brother, and my potna Jay fenna go get this Schrimage game popn' at Pratola gym."

"I didn't know you knew how to play basketball."

"It's a lot you don't know about me."

"Same here," Coco said. "I guess we finna get real acquainted."

"I guess so," Young Money answered back. "But look, I'm fenna get ready to slide to the gym. I'm hit you later."

"All right, it was nice talking to you, in y'all betta win."

"That's all I do is win."

"Yea, we gon' see."

As Young Money was getting ready to leave, he bumped into his mom, Pam. "Wassup, Ma, where you been at?"

"Minding my business in staying out of yours." And she headed to her room for some much-needed sleep.

"Ayy, Money, call dat nigga YM," Jay had said after he finished rolling up the wood they was gon' smoke after the game.

"There, that nigga go right there," Money said.

"Wassup wit' you, niggas," Young Money said as he was getting in the back seat.

On the way to the gym, Young Money got a text from TaTa. "Wassup, babe? What you doing?" He looked at his phone and put it back in his pocket.

"Jay, pass the rock," Young Money said and lined up on for the game-winning shot—the three-point line—as Jay passed the ball. Young Money pulled up from the three for the win.

As they was sitting on the bleachers, catching their breath and talking 'bout the game, "A, Money, you seen that nigga Young Money?" Jay said. "Nigga thought he was Clay Thompson."

Money started laughing. "You niggas know wassup."

"Ayy, let me holla at ya'll about som'thing," Young Money said.

"What?" both Jay and Money said at the same time.

"All right, look, I'ma keep it all the way a hunned wit' you niggas. I'm tryna get paid in. I ain't getting no job. I'ma take what I want, so is you niggas in or not?" Young Money looked at Jay and Money.

"We list'ning, nigga. Talk," Jay said.

"Aight, look, I'm break this shit down as simple as possible. I was choppin' it up with my big cousin Shota, and he put me onto a paper route. Now look, it consists of us breaking into houses."

"Wait a minute," Money said. "So yo want as to run into some houses? That sound like some dopefiend shit."

"Nigga, that ain't no dopefiend shit," Young Money said. "How the fuck you think that nigga Shota eating by hitting houses in I'm tryna eat just like that? So like I was saying, we gon' hit a few spots in run it up. Just follow my lead, and we gon' get that bag. So wassup? Y'all niggas in or what?"

"Fuck it, I'm in," Jay said.

Young Money looked at Money. "I'm telling you right now, YM, if this shit backfire, I'm beatn' yo ass. I'm in too."

"All right, look, I'ma need one favour," Young Money told Money.

"In what's that?"

"Ask that bitch Danyale to get us a rental. You know you gotta be twenty-five in up to get one."

"It's good. Say no more. I got chu."

"All right, gentleman, meeting adjourned."

"Okay, look at you, Mulan. I just slayed yo shit," Fendi had said out loud.

"You definitely did yo thang."

"So where y'all going?" Fendi said as she was finishing flat-ironing Mulan's hair. This was a new look for Coco. Fendi had done her hair with a part down the middle. She usually wore it naturally curly.

"We fenna go to Dave & Buster."

"Dave & Busters?" Fendi repeated with a stale face.

"Yea, bitch, is it something wrong with that?"

"I'm just saying o boy couldn't take you nowhere exclusive?"

"Everybody not bougie like you."

"Bitch, I'm not bougie. I just got high standards."

"Yea, whatever. Anyway, I need to use yo ID. I'm tryna get some drinks in. You know I don't turn twenty-one till next year."

"Girl, you act like that's hella faraway. That's in the next ninety days," Fendi said.

"I know. I'm fenna be that big twenty-one. Time be movin' so fast."

"You need to let somebody hit that shit before you turn around and be old as dirt, and ain't nobody gon' want that shit."

"Bitch, somebody gon' always want this."

"Who? Young Money?" Fendi said.

"I ain't even trippin' off him like that."

"Girl, stop lyin'. You been talking 'bout that boy since I been doing yo hair."

"Why you putting extra on it all? All I said was I thought he was cute"

"I ain't gon' lie, I'm feelin' him. It's just something about him."

"Well, I'm fenna get ready to go."

Fendi said, "Call me in give me all the details on yo lil date."

"Will do," Mulan said.

Young Money was fresh out the shower. As he was getting ready to get dressed, his phone rung. "Hello, what's good?"

"Not you, nigga. Why the fuck you ain't text me back earlier?" TaTa said.

"I was busy."

"Busy doing what you probelly was fucking with that bitch Lexus."

"Man, bitch, get the fuck out of here with that shit. Wassup though? What you want?"

"You know what I want. I need some dick. Is it good?"

Click. Young Money hung up the phone and blocked TaTa from calling him for that day. He didn't need no interruptions on his date wit Mulan. He was tryna bend her shit over, but little did he know it was gon' be easier said than done. Once he was done getting dressed, he looked at himself over in the mirror. He had on an all-red Supreme shirt, some all-black True Religion jeans with the all-red Jordan Fives. Satisfied with his look, he picked up the phone to FaceTime Mulan.

Ring, ring, ring. "Hello," Mulan said.

"Wassup, beautiful? What you got going on?"

"Finishing up my makeup."

"Look at you tryna get all fancy and shit. I see you."

"You know nothing too much. Oh, and I'ma be on my way in thirty minutes."

"A'ight, I'ma see you when you get here."

Mulan pulled up to the address Young Money gave her. She said to herself, "It look grimey over here." She hurried up and called Young Money. Ring, ring, ring. "I'm outside." As Young Money was walking to her car, she was checking his swag out. "Okay, he looking fresh." Young Money hopped in the car, and they pulled off. Once they bent a few corners, he told her to put on that new song by Ice and DrewBeez. "What's that murda music?"

"Yea, that one." As the song was playing, Young Money rolled up a back wood and cired up. After he inhaled the cookies, he asked Mulan if she smoked. "Yea, I smoke, knowing she don't even be smoking like that." As she inhaled the cookies, she got an instant buzz. Once they made it to Dave & Buster's, the scene was low-key lit. "You want anything to drink?" Mulan said.

"Something to drink as in what?"

"Some alcohol, boy."

"Okay, since we fucking wit' it like that, get me some Hennessy."

"Okay, I'ma get me a strawberry daiquiri with a shot of tequila. And

I wants some chicken strips with some ranch sauce. What you getting?" she asked Young Money.

"I'm fenna get these chicken and steak quesadillas." They ordered their food.

"So, Young Money, so how do you see me in you building this friendship?"

As he was fenna answer her question, the drinks came. He took a sip of his Henny. "I mean, you cool like when I first saw you, I told myself, 'I gotta get to know this girl,' and I think you cute."

"Awww, that was nice. I think you cute too, and I want to get to know you more, so let's toast to getting to know each other."

After three drinks apiece and all the arcade games they played to last a lifetime, they were ready to leave on the way back to the car. "I really enjoyed myself tonight," Mulan had said.

"You was supposed to when you fucking with a real nigga like me. You gon' always enjoy yo'self."

"Look at you tryna run game. I'm hearing you, though. I am fortunate enough to meet someone like the last nigga I tried to get to know. He was liar and cheater. So please don't lie to me. Just always keep it a hunned with me."

"I'm definitely gon' do that. It's all good. I'm fillin' you anyway you fenna be, babe."

"Oh, am I you sure you don't already have one of those?"

"Nah, none of those. A few lil booty calls, that's it. Yea, about that, once I make you my nigga, all yo lil hoes, you got that shit gon' come to a end." Young Money chuckled.

"Ain't shit funny. I'm serious."

"I hear you." As they reached Young Money's house, Mulan had parked.

"I really did enjoy myself," she had said once again.

"So when I'ma get to see you again?"

"Whenever you want to."

"Ooh, don't say that because I a be over here every day looking for that ass."

"Nah, I'm just playin'. I'ma figure it out because I be busy throughout the week."

"It's all good. Just tap in."

"All right."

Young Money leaned over and gave her a kiss on the cheek and got out the car. "Call me once you make it in," Young Money told her.

"All right, I will. You betta pick up the phone when I call."

"I got chu."

"Ayy, Money, look at this nigga Young Money slipn'," Jay said. "Hunk the horn at that nigga." Honk, honk. Young Money looked towards where the noise was coming from and saw that it was Jay and his brother.

"Man, you niggas play hella much. Had a nigga spooked."

"Let me find out dude was fenna shit on hisself," Money said.

"Fuck ya'll."

"Ayy, who was that girl that just dropped you off?" Jay asked him.

"Oh, that was baby I knocked at the WingStop that day."

"I seen yo ass all cupped cocked up in shit," Money told him.

"Man, fuck all that shit. You niggas ready to get paid because a nigga like me tryna get that bag."

"We waiting on you nigga call the play," Jay answered.

"Aight, so look, we gon' bust our move Monday morning. Money, did you holla at Danyale about the wip?"

"Yea, she said she gon' get it tomorrow."

"Aight, that's wassup. We in motion," Young Money said. "So look, this the play. Jay, you gon' be the driver. Yo job is to make sure ain't nobody drivin' up in down the street and make sure ain't no police in the area." Jay shook his head to let Young Money know that he agree on what he just said. "Now look, Money, me and you gon' go in the spot. We only looking for cash in jewelry and any Apple electronics. That's it, and that's all."

"It's all good. I got you."

"Aight, I'ma tap in with you niggas later. I'm fenna line me some Bunz up."

"Fuck you, dry-ass niggas fenna do."

"Shit, I'm fenna do the same shit," Jay said. "What about you, Money?"

"You know me. I'm fenna go to my babe house."

"Who? Danyale?" Young Money said.

"You know it, and she just cooked something fat for a nigga."

"Well, I see you pussys later." Young Money got out the car and walked to the house.

As he was walking in, he saw TaTa walking toward him. "So that's what we doing muthafuckas putn me on block and shit."

"So what, bitch, got you actn' brand-new."

"Let me find out. It's one of these bitches around here I'ma fuck one of they ass up straight up."

"You done?" Young Money said.

"No, I'm not done. Here I am being faithful to yo dog ass, and you can't even appreciate that."

"Faithful? Bitch, get the fuck out of here. You was just fucking on that nigga G-Mann from Big Block."

"No, the fuck I don't. I been stop fucking with that nigga. It's been all about you, so stop fucking playing with me like you don't know wassup."

"Man, miss me wit all that shit. I'm fenna go lay down. Go get me some cooks from dat nigga Shota."

"What you want me to get you?"

"Get me a quarter and some woods."

"All right, babe, I be back in a minute."

"Yea, I hear you." Young Money finally made it in the house, and as soon as he did, his phone rung. Once he seen who was calling, he had a smile on his face.

"What's popn'?" Mulan said.

"Check you out tryna sound like me. I ain't doing shit colln' you. Just got in the house."

"Yea, I had stopped at my cousin's house. I had a few drinks and shit, but they was fenna go out to the club, in I don't do the club all like that, so I'm at home with nothing to do, bored out my mind. I'm about to hop in the shower in watch my web series on YouTube. I was just calling to let you know I made it in."

"Aight, just hit me once you get out the shower. All right, I'll call you later."

Knock, knock, knock. "Damn, what took you so long to open the door?" TaTa said as she walked in the house. "Huh?" as she handed him his cookies and woods.

TaTa walked to Young Money's room and began stripping her clothes off. She left nothing but her red lace see-through boy shorts on and laid on top of Young Money's bed on her stomach. She knew what she was doing. She was tryna show Young Money her beautiful figure. "I see you don't waste no time. You done made yoself all comfortable in shit."

"Boy, stop playin' with me, you know. Wassup? This my bed. I'm the only bitch that's gon' be laying in this bed. Yea, that part."

"Bitch, you siked out," Young Money said as he was rolling up the wood. Tata started movin' both her ass cheeks; as she was lying down on her stomach, she seen Young Money staring at her.

"You like when I make my ass jump."

"Fuck yea, do it again." As TaTa did it again, Young Money started rubbing and grabbing on her ass. TaTa loved when he did that. After he hit the blunt a few times, he passed it to TaTa.

She hit the blunt and asked Young Money, "When you gon' start taking me serious? I mean, we ben fucking with each other on in off since we was fifteen. Here it is. We grown now, and you still on that same as shit."

"My niggas, pass the fucking wood. This bitch always in her feeling when she get high."

"That's all you got to say is pass the wood. You know what? Fuck you in this wood." TaTa threw the wood across the room and got up to leave. As she was getting dressed, Young Money started laughing.

"Use a siked out as bitch. For real, you bipolar is fuck," he said as he continued to laugh.

"Oh, it's funny? It ain't gon' be funny when I'm gone in where you gon' go."

"Out you life. I promise you that yea, that's what you always in. You always come back to daddy dick."

"Ooh, I fucking hate you," she said as she walked out the door. Young Money went to go pick the wood up, sparked it back up, and inhaled the cookie smoke.

"O stupid-ass bitch," he said to no one in particular as he was thinking about how Monday was gon' play out.

"So look, everybody know they position. We don't need no mistakes," Young Money said to Jay in Money.

"Nigga, we know what the fuck to do. You told us the play about a thousand times," Jay said.

"Aight, let's go get this bag," Young Money said out loud.

On the way to the avenues, everybody was in deep thought. The avenues was where all the upper class lived. "Ayy, Jay, make a left right here," Young Money said. "All right, stop right here." Young Money hopped out the car, looking like an electrician. He had the whole getup with the hat and the clipboard. As he approached the house, he knocked three different times and waited like two minutes; nobody came to the door. Once he saw that, he took the crowbar out his pants and put the crowbar in between the crack of the door where the knob was. At once, he wiggled the crowbar thru the door, then it popped open. He signaled to Money that the coast is clear. Young Money and Money were running through the house, flipping over mattresses and opening drawers.

"I found it," Young Money said.

"What? Oh, shit, how much money is that?"

"I don't know, but grab that jewelry box."

Ring, ring. "What's good? You niggas ready?" Jay said.

"Yea, is it good to come out?"

"Yea, it's good." Money and Young Money came walking out the house towards the car. Once they got in the car, Jay asked Mulan if they got anything.

"Just drive off, then we gon' holla once we get back to the house. Pull over right here real quick." Young Money wiped the jewelry box off and threw it out the window. As Jay pulled up to his house, they all got out the car and walked in the house.

"Nigga, we on," Young Money said excitedly as he pulled the money out his pocket and threw it on the table.

"Let's count this money," Jay said.

Money had emptied the jewelry he had gotten out the house on the table. Young Money started counting the money. "Damn, bra, look at all Mulan blue strips," Money said.

"Ayy, day roll up some dro," Young Money said as he continued to count the money. Once he got done, the total amount came out to $25,000. "So look, the count came out to $25,000 dollas, so we get $8,300 hundred apiece and plus the jewelry. Today was a good day, I might say," Young Money said as he hit the wood and gave everybody their cut.

"So what we gonna do with the jewelry?" Money asked.

"I'ma go holla at Shota. He got somebody who gon' buy all that shit," Young Money said.

"I wonder how much all that jewelry worth," Jay said.

"Whatever it's worth, we gon' get paid straight up," Young Money told them.

"Ayy, Jay, take a picture of me real quick. I'm fenna flex on these brake niggas on the gram. There you go with that hot shit," Money said.

"My nigga, fuck what you talking right now? I'm fenna show Mulan hoes I got dat bag on me straight up."

Jay took the pic. After that, Young Money gathered up the jewelry and was getting ready to learn until Money told him to come holla at him real quick. "What's good, bruh?" Young Money had that look on his face like he can give two fucks what Money had to say.

"Look, my nigga, I know you feeln' yoself right now, but I'ma let you know right now I'm not going to jail over yo stupidity."

"Yea, I hear you."

"You done, nigga, because I got shit to do." After that, Money just shook his head and said to himself, "O dumbass nigga."

Young Money sat on his bed, counting his money over and over again. He thought to hisself, *Man, I ain't never had this much money ever. What the fuck I'm fenna buy first? I'ma get a Forarri. Nah, I can't get no Forarri. I ain't got enough money for that shit. Fuck it, I'ma just holla at big cuz in, see where I can get a nice whip.* Ring, ring, ring. "What's popn'?" Money said to the person who just FaceTimed him.

"Young Money, I miss you, baby," Red said in her ratchet Cardi B voice.

"Bitch, you phony. I been tryna tap in with you. Where the fuck yo antanas been at?"

"They been right here with you."

"Say anything. What's good though? Nothing been missing you tryna see you in stuff."

"Yea, aight, I'm fenna go bust this move. I'ma tap in with you, which I'm done all right, babe. You betta call me because I need my issue." Young Money hung up the phone. Ol' thirsty-ass bitch. He counted his money once again. Them crispy blue hunneds felt good in his hands.

"I need to call this nigga Shota," he said to no one in particular. Ring, ring. "Wassup, lil cuz? What's it's hittn for?"

"All man it's hittn' for a whole lot. Pull up to Mom's house, aight? I'm fenna be on my way."

"Aight." As Money was chillin', he texted Mulan.

"Wassup, beautiful?"

"Nothing, ready to get off work. What you up 2?"

"Shit, chillin'. I was just thinking 'bout you."

"Aww, how nice of you. I feel special. I see we got jokes. Nah, I'm just playin wit you. I been thinking 'bout you too."

When I'ma get to see you again?"

Mulan texted back, "Whenever you want too. How bout tonight once I get off work?"

"Aight, just hit me [with kiss heart face emoji] [kissy face emoji]."

"Man, where the fuck this nigga at?" Knock, knock. "Damn, nigga, took you long enough."

"My bad, lil cuzn. I had to make a pit stop real quick, went to go see this smart chick 'bout some brain. You know how that be," Shota said.

"Yea, I hear you, my nigga. You wild," Young Money said with a grin on her face.

"So where that orange chicken at?" *Orange chicken* was their slang for twenty-four-karat gold.

"Oh, that shit in my room. I'm telln' you, I did my thang on my first lick." Young Money grabbed his bankroll and showed it to Shota.

"Okay, I see who getting money. How much y'all came up with?"

"Like twenty-five bands and that jewelry right there."

Shota knew how to add and subtract money, so good he easily said, "8,300 apiece. Not bad for yo first lick. So look, I'ma go holla at my people in I'ma get at you tonight."

"Aight, tap in wit me later."

Money walked in the house ans went straight to his room. Young Money walked right in Money's room behind him, smoking on some cookies. "Wassup, pussy? You still in yo feeling?" he said, passing the wood to Money.

Money took the wood and inhaled the cookie smoke and said, "Do you? I ain't tripn'. But I'm saying you act like you my older brother. We came out of Moma stomach at the same time. Remember, she had to get a C-section, man. Gone wit that bullshit," Money said.

"Check it out, though. I just got through holln' at Shota. And he like he fenna go holla at his people to see how much that gold worth, so once he get back at me, I'ma holla at you in Jay in give y'all yo cut."

"Aight." Young Money walked towards the door, but before he left out, he told Money he loved him. "I love you too, bra, no homo. Ayy, YM, let me get a wood."

"Come on, my nigga. How you ain't got no woods?"

"Because, nigga, I don't." Young Money couldn't do nothing but shake his head and threw him a wood.

"This got damn pharmacy job getting played out got a bitch slaving for thirteen dollas a hour. A bitch can't even pay her rent if it wasn't for me stealing them oxycontin and that promethazine with codeine to sell. I don't know what I would do," Mulan said, thinking to herself. She wished her mom was still alive. She passed when Mulan was sixteen due to her heavy chain smoking. Her mom would go through one or two packs a day, which caused her cancer, and she only had thirty days to live. Mulan spent each day by her mother's side. One day after school, she went to her mom's room to show her how she did on her final exam. "Mom, guess what? I got an A+ on my final. Ain't you proud of yo daughter, Moma?" As she walked towards her mom, she seen that she wasn't breathing. "O my god, Moma, no, you can't leave me right now. I need you. I don't have nobody else." Mulan called air in to tell them what happened. She called her grandmother, and her mom's mother told her what happened, and she had the nerve to say, "I told your mom if she had you, she was gon' have nothing but bad luck, so therefore, I don't want nothing to do with y'all," and hung up the phone. Mulan had to get her dad's side of the family to help get her mom buried traditionally. Ever since that day, she resented everybody on her mom's side of the family. Once she came back to reality, she wiped the tears from her face and started up her car and headed home. Once she got home, she thought about Young Money, and that put a smile on her face, so she decided to call him. "Wassup, big head?"

"Oh, I'm a big head? I got a big head for you, or you only knew."

"What was that you just said, boy?"

"Nothing," Young Money said, smiling. "Wassup with you though? How was yo day at work?"

"Long, tiring, long. Did I say long? So yea, you get the picture. I show be glad when I get my medical certificate to qualify for this RN position at Kaiser Hospital."

"O yea, that's wassup," Young Money said. "I like the fact that you tryna do something with yo life."

"O, you like the fact I got a good head on my shoulders and I ain't ran through like a lot or these bitches out here."

"Yea, that part," Young Money said.

"Well, I'ma be on my way in a minute. I'm fenna hop in the shower and get dressed.

"Aight, I'ma see you when you get here."

Young Money looked at the time. It was going on 9:30 p.m. "Let me call this nigga."

"What's pop'n'?" Shota said into the phone.

"Shit, I'm tryna see wassup with that orange chicken, what it's hittn foe?"

"Ayy, look, y'all did y'all thang. I'm coming around the corner right now. Unlock the door."

Shota came in the house wit a Gucci backpack full of money. They sat down in the living room, and Shota tossed the backpack to Young Money. "How much is this?"

"Nigga, count it in." See, Shota took a wood out, broke it down, and rolled up some cookies.

After Young Money counted all the money, he jumped up and down, yelling, "This $50,000 dollas, nigga. We on. Fuck yea, that's what I'm talking 'bout. Let me hit that wood." Shota passed the cookies to him.

"Look, lil nigga, don't be spending all yo money at once. Get what you need and put the rest up."

"Shit, I need a lot. First thing first, I need a whip thang. I need a cannon."

Wait, wait, what you need a gun for?"

"Man, you know how shit be out here."

"Yea, I hear you. Well, look, I'ma see what I can do 'bout that cannon. As far as the car, my people got a car lot, nothing but foreign whips, but you betta be ready to spend."

"Come on, man. My money good. You see, I got that bag on me."

"Aight, then I'ma tap in with you later. I got some pussy on deck." Young Money sat back down and was in awe of what he was looking at.

"Now this is what the fuck I'm talking 'bout. This real money," he said as he put everybody's cut to the side; it was an even split $17,500 apiece. He opened Money's door and tossed him his money "Say thank you," Young Money said.

"What, nigga? Get the fuck out a here. We in this shit together."

"Nah, I'm just fucking wit you, but look, check it out. We just made $25,000 apiece, you in me. Ain't never seen this kind of money."

"I ain't gon' lie, we on to something good.

I say we bust a move like this every week, 'bout time the summer over, we gon' have hella money put up, so wassup, that's the plan."

"Hell yea, that's the plan," Money said.

"Ayy, call dat nigga Jay in. Tell him to come get his doe. Matter of fact, I'm fenna FaceTime him." Ring, ring. Wassup wit my round fuck you got going on."

"Shit, at this bitch Ashley house."

"O yea? Well, nigga, you bullshitn'. We just cashed in on that orange chicken." Young Money showed him the stacks of money. "Ayy, Money, show that nigga you got that bag on you." Money showed Jay the stacks of money.

"You betta pull up 'fore I spend yo shit on a bust-down chain," Money said.

"Nigga, you ain't crazy. You know wassup, but I'm fenna be on my way right now."

"Aight, we gon' be here."

As Young Money hung up the phone, he asked Money what the first thing he was gon' get with his doe. "You know me, I'm tryna come foreign."

"Ayy, that's crazy, my nigga. I was thinking the same shit. They say great minds think alike."

"So since you tryna get a whip, you might as well come with me in Shota in the morning to the car lot."

"Yep, it's all good. I'm definitely coming."

"Aight, fenna get up outa here. I'm fenna go fuck with my foreign bitch. I'm a pick her up in my foreign whip ha ha ha. I should be a rapper, huh."

"Get the fuck out of here. You know you can't rap," Money said.

Young Money left out the room to get dressed.

Mulan was on her way out the door; she was feeln' her lil look. She had her hair in a high B ponytail, edges on point. She had on a red crop top shirt with some washed destroyed jeans, some red bottoms, and her Louis Vuitton handbag. She gave herself the okay and headed to her car. On her way to pick up Young Money, she was slapn' that cutthroat album by Yatta. Ring, ring. "I'm outside."

"Aight, I'm coming out right now."

As Young Money was approaching her car, Mulan was checking him out. *Damn, this nigga fine as fuck.* Young Money hopped in the car.

"You smell good. Who you tryna impress?"

"Boy, stop. I do this on a regular. Let me find out them lil bitches you call yo friends be having a lil odor to them."

"Ahaha, you hella funny," Young Money told her.

"So what you tryna do?" Mulan asked Young Money.

"Shit, it's whatever. I'm just tryna chill wit you."

"Ooh, I know where we can go. We can go to Monkey King. It's a Chinese food restaurant in Alameda."

"Okay, dat's wassup. I ain't been there before."

"Oh, you haven't? I would of thought one of yo lil friends would of took you."

"Here you go with the jokes again."

"Nah, let me stop. I'ma stall you out for now."

Once they got to Monkey King, it was a fifteen-minute wait. Young Money's phone rung; it was TaTa. Mulan was looking at him like, "You not gon' answer it?"

"Nah, it ain't important to me."

"So what's important to you then?"

"You and I are enjoying ourselves."

"Good answer," Mulan said.

"Table 3 is ready for a party of two."

"Come on, That's us," Mulan said. They sat down, and the waiter came and asked them if they were ready to order. "Um, can you give us a few minutes? Thank you," Mulan said. "So what you gon' order?"

"I'm tryna figure that out," Money said.

"Well, I'm fenna get some dry fried ribs and some shrimp fried rice."

"Shit, I'ma get um some beef in broccoli, some shrimp fried rice, and some jumbo breaded prawns with some sweet in sour sauce."

"Damn, boy, you tryna get yo eat on."

"You know a nigga gotta get his eat on."

"Are you guys ready to order now?" Mulan and Young Money gave the water their order. "Okay, your food will be here shortly."

"Thank you," Mulan said. "So, Mr. Young Money, this is our second date, and we barely still know each other."

"What else do you feel like you need to know?"

"Well, for starters, I wanna know how it is that yo real name is Young Money."

"My dad was a big-time drug dealer, and he loved money, and people that knew him called him Big Money, so once he found out he was having twin boys, he told my mom that he wanted our names to be Money and Young Money, but before we were born, my dad got killed."

"Oh my god, I am so sorry," Mulan said.

"It's all good. It ain't yo fault, but like I was saying, my mom knew that my dad wanted our names to be what he had told her before he died, so that's my story, in I'm sticking to it." He laughed it off to lighten the mood.

The food came, and they ate and got to know each other a lot more. Once the bill came, Mulan was reaching for her credit card. But Young

Money told her he got it and pulled out a bank roll and paid for the bill. "You ready?"

"Yea, I'm ready," Mulan said.

Once they got in the car, Young Money leaned his seat back. "Man, I'm full as fuck."

"I bet you is. All that food you ate could of feed a whole village."

"Yea, I hear you."

Mulan put in that new I'ma CD and went to her favorite song. She started singing along the lyrics. Young Money was rolling up a wood to get his smoke on; he hit it a few times. "Mulan, you tryna hit this."

She grabbed the wood still in sync with the song. Mulan pulled up to her apartment, and she had a nice lil one-bedroom in Lake Ment. "You wanna come up? Unless you got to check in or something."

"Nah, it's all about you right now."

"You in yo lil comebacks."

You got an answer for everything, in you smoking up all me dro, pass the wood."

"Oh, my bad," Mulan said, chuckling. "I must be feelin' myself. I'm just over here puffin away." Once they got in the spot, Mulan said, "Make yourself at home," and walked to her room to put something on more comfortable. She came out in some cotton boy's shorts with a white tank top. Young Money couldn't help but stare at her physique. "You like what you see," Mulan said as she was walking to her refrigerator to get something to drink. She poured herself some fruit punch Minute Maid. "You want something to drink?" she asked Young Money.

"Yea." As Mulan was walking towards him, he was checking out her feet. (Okay, she got some pretty feet.) She sat on the couch next to Young Money and put a movie on. As she scooted next to Young Money, he put his arm around her so she could lay her head on his shoulder. Ten minutes in the movie, Young Money took his arm from around her and placed it by her waist. She peeped his move; she wanted to see how far he was gon' take it. Once he did that, he let his hand to her ass; he had to touch it. Seeing her in them boy shorts was driving him crazy. As he started to rub and feel on her ass, Mulan said, "You like that? That ass soft, huh."

"Hell yea, that shit soft." Young Money said fuck it and started kissing her. Once he did that, it took Mulan by surprise, but she accepted the kiss and slid her tongue in his mouth. They were kissing like it was their last kiss on earth. Mulan got on top of Young Money, and he was gripping her ass as they were continuing kissing. He slid his fingers in her pussy and rubbed on her clit. Mulan began to moan. "Oooh o my god umm huhh you . . . gon' mence me. Oooh, I'm fenna come." Young Money flipped her over on the couch, and he started to take his clothes off. "Wait, I gotta tell you something."

"What that? You ready for this dick?"

"Um, not quiet. I mean, I'm ready but just not right now. I'ma virgin."

"What? Get the fuck outa here. You ain't no virgin."

"I put dat on my dead mother. I'ma virgin. Watch you a see if you make it."

"So you really are a virgin. I thought them were extinct."

That made her laugh. "Not every female is out there like that."

"O yea, I mean, it's all good. I'm not in no rush. Whenever you ready. What we have is bigger than sex."

"You mean that so you still want to continue to build our relationship?"

"Of course."

After that, they stayed up talking, and she fell asleep in his arms. Morning came. "Fuck, I'm fenna be late for school. Young Money, wake up."

"Man, what time is it?"

"It's eight a.m. That means I gotta take a shower, get dressed, and be at school to drop you off all in thirty minutes. Why don't you just get in the shower and get dressed, and I'ma just have my cousin to come get me, and that way, you won't be late for school."

"Sounds like a plan to me," Mulan said.

Once Mulan finished getting ready, she was on her way out the door. "It's food in the refrigerator, so if you hungry, you can make you something to eat." She gave him a kiss. As she was walking off, Young Money slapped her on her ass. "Oow, you play too much."

"Have a nice day at school, babe."

"Aight, you too." Mulan headed off to school. Young Money sat back on the couch, soaking everything in. (*Damn, baby a virgin. That's crazy. I ain't never had no virgin pussy. I'm definitely tryna see what that be like.*)

He walked to the refrigerator and poured him some orange juice and turned on the news. "This is Channel 5 news, bringing breaking news. It was a double homicide in Bayview Hunters Point on Third in Kirkwood. It was told that no one could ID the suspects, so therefore, San Francisco PD has no leads. Back to you, Bill."

"Man, that's crazy," Young Money said to no one in particular. *That's two for the home team*, he thought with a smile on his face. He picked up his phone and called Shota. Ring, ring. "Hello," Shota said, sounding all sleepy. "What's good?"

"Nigga, it's like asine something in the morning. Tha fuck you up so early for?"

"I don't know. I couldn't sleep, and I stayed at my bitch's house."

Where you at right now?"

"I'm in the town by Lake Merrit."

"Aight, look, I'm get up in a minute, and I'ma come get you in take you to go get yo whip."

"You might as well grab Money too. He tryna get a whip too."

"Aight, I'ma tap in with you, nigga." Young Money hung up the phone. He dozed off and woke up to his phone ringing. "What's good, my nigga?"

"Shit on 580 right now. Text me the address."

"Aight, I'm fenna send it to you right now."

Young Money got up and went to the bathroom. He went to go take a piss and saw some mouthwash and poured some in his mouth and gargled it and rinsed his mouth out. He got a text from Shota. "I'm outside nigga." Young Money looked at the door and headed to the car. Once he got in, Shota pulled off. "I hope you got yo money right," Shota told him.

"Nigga, my money good. Money, show this nigga we got that bag on us."

Money took the stacks of money out his Nike sweatpants and handed Young Money his doe. "Fuck you mean if my money right. Ayy, Money, I'm fenna go live. Put me on the gram."

Here this nigga go again, Money thought. Young Money started talking his shit wit the stacks of money to his ear.

As they was pullin' up to the car lot, he grabbed his phone from Young Money and continued to be online. "Yea, man, I'm fenna cop me som'thing foreign on you broke niggas. You gon' see me pull up clean, but I'ma get at y'all later though." Once Young Money finally got off the phone, he saw how many clean wipes they had, but he already had his mind made up on what he wanted. He was tryna get a Porsche Panamera, and he was willing to spend every last dolla he had in his pocket on one.

"You seen anything you like?" Shota asked Young Money.

"Yeah, I'm feelin' that Porsche Panamera."

"O yea, you know how much one of them going for. That's 2013 panny, dude. Gon' want at least forty-five bands. You might as well get something in yo range. Look at this infinity. It's a M45. Them bitches run, and it's 2012. I can talk to Felipe, and I can get him to give it to you for the low."

"I mean, it's clean in all, but I really want that Porsche. I tell you what stack yo doe in we can come back in get that Panamera you want."

"I'ma tell Filipe to hold it for you."

"Aight, that's cool," Young Money said.

"Money, you seen something you like?" Shota asked him.

"Hell yeah, I'm feelin that Infiniti Coupe."

"Aight, I'm fenna go holla at yo boy right now."

When Shota came back out with both pink slips, he said, "Young Money, huh, I got yo shit for like 10,500 money. Ours came up to 12,000. Y'all just gotta sign this paperwork to give him y'all money."

As they finished signing the forms, they both counted out the amount of money they needed for their whips. "Wassup, my friend," Filipe said. "So you guys like the Infinities."

"I mean, they cool," Young Money said. "But I really want that Porsche Panamera.

"O yea, Shota was telling me something about that. I told him I'ma hold it for you."

"Yea, you do that because I'm definitely coming back to get that."

Money and Young Money cashed out on they whips. And Filipe had tossed them their keys. As Young Money and Money got in, they whips, they both looked at each other. "Let's race, aight, but look, whoever win gotta give up a bund."

"Aight, bet."

They both started their cars up, and both pulled off. Young Money yanked off first. He was in the lead, but Money was in a stick, so once he started playing with the clutch, he blew past Young Money.

Ring, ring. "Wassup, big cuzn?"

"The fuck you lil niggas doing? Y'all ready to get pulled over by the police already."

"Nah, me in this nigga Money had a bet to see who car is faster."

"Aight, well, fall back off that shit, but anyway, y'all tryna go get something to eat."

"Yea, we're you tryna go?"

"I was thinking Ruth Chris."

"Ain't that that one spot were the food coast hella much."

"Yea, som'thing like that. Y'all lil niggas coming or not? I'm fenna meet my lil bitch there."

"Yea, we comin."

"Aight, follow me."

Young Money FacedTimed Money. "Ayy, bra, follow me. We fenna follow this nigga Shota to Ruth Chris. Aight, it's good."

Once they got to Ruth Chris, they got seated. "Y'all ain't gon' introduce yourselves to my girl?"

"Oh, my bad. I'm Young Money."

"And I'm Money."

"Nice to meet both you guys, but wait, y'all twins or something?"

They both looked at each other. "Yea, we twins."

"Oh, how cute. I bet y'all get all the girls."

"I do," Young Money said, pointing at himself. "I don't know 'bout him," he said, looking at Money.

"Nigga, I don't know why you saying anything. You know I get bitches."

"Fall back with that shit," Shota said.

The waiter approached their table. "Are you ready to order?"

"Yes, I will like the stuffed chicken with crab macaroni and cheese and a glass of rosey," Shota said.

"What about for you two gentlemen?"

"Can I get som'thing wit some steak," Young Money said.

"Well, we have a steak special that comes wit a filet me yong steak with a fully loaded baked potato, a side order of some jumbo prawns, and to finish it off with some asparagus. How does that sound?"

"Shit, that sound good as fuck."

The lady smiled. "And how 'bout you, young man?"

"I will have the same thing too."

"And for the lady?"

"Can you just give me a glass of wine and a chicken in shrimp salad."

"Will that be all?"

"Yes, that will be all."

"Okay, your food will be coming shortly."

"Woooh, I'm stuffed," Money said. "Ayy, YM, fire up. I'm tryna get high."

"The fuck you doing, Young Money? Don't fire dat shit up. Up in here, this is not the trap house, bra. Wait till you get outside."

"All right, come on, Money. We fenna cut as they was getting up to leave."

Shota said, "Ain't ya'll forgetting something?"

They both looked at each other and said, "No, man. Stop fucking playing with me. Ya'll betta pay y'all tab."

"Shit, we thought you had it, big baller."

"Nah, ya'll two niggas the ballers."

"Nah, we just fucking around. How much I owe both ya'll niggas?"

Shit came up to $200 dollars apiece. They paid for their meals and left. Once they got to their cars, they smoked and got in there whips. "You wanna bet back," Money said.

"Nah, I'm good. I'm fenna just slide back to the projects."

"Man, fuck all that. We just got are whips. I ain't tryna be posted in the hood like that."

"So what you tryna do?" Young Money said.

"I got some hoes on deck, and she got a auntie that's bad. She only like twenty-one, and her niece eighteen, so wassup, you tryna fuck with it?"

"Hell yea, but let's bend a lap through the point, and before we slide to the moe, we gon' grab some duce from the Q-street store, aight bet?"

When they got on the freeway, Money and Young Money were profiling in and out of Kines. Once they made it back to the point, they slid through every project in the hood, stopped, and grabbed the duce and some more cookies and headed to the Fillmore District, which was west from Hunters Point. It took no more than ten minutes to get there. Once they pulled up to MacArthur, a.k.a. Mankind Block, Money FaceTimed Stacy. Ring, ring. "Wassup, babe? Where you at?"

"I'm outside. Unlock the door."

"All right, yo brought some drank?"

"Yep, ayy yo auntie there."

"No, why? Let me find out you checkn' for my untie."

"Not even I was gon' put my brother Young Money on wit her."

"Un ahh, don't he fuck wit dat girl TaTa."

"Man, fuck nah."

"That ain't what I heard, but anyway, my right hand here."

"In who is yo right hand?"

"Mi-Mi that went to school wit us."

"O yea, sho cool."

"Open the door. I'm fenna come in."

"So what's the deal? What it's hittn' foe?" Young Money said as he took a waterfall from the duce.

"It's good, but her auntie untigin in there. Her potna Mi-Mi is thow, and she bad."

"Aight, say no more."

Once they made it into the apartment, Money went to go sit down by Stacy.

"You don't know nobody, Young Money."

"Wassup, Stace?"

"Ooh, you be acting phoney just because me and TaTa don't get along. Don't mean you gotta act like that."

"Man gone wit that shit. You siked out."

"Can I hit yo bottle though?" Stacy asked him.

"Yep, it's good."

He passed the bottle to Money first, and Money hit it and gave it to her. Once the bottle went around a few times, Stacy was feelin' herself. She was like, "Wassup, right hand? Let's do are shit."

Mi-Mi was like, "You ain't ready, right hand. Fuck it. Come on. Let's fuck it up."

Stacy put some music on, and they both started twerkin'. Money and Young Money were passing the wood back to each other, watching the show in front of them. Young Money took out his phone and put them on Snapchat. His caption said, "These bitches ready to fuck something." Once they was finished, they both fell on the couch laughing. Once Mi-Mi caught her breath, she started twerkin' on Young Money. Stacy was like, "Fuck it up, right hand," as she was hittin' the wood siting on Money's lap.

Money was whispering in her ear, "Wassup, let's go to yo room, Stacy." And Money walked to her room.

"Ooh, y'all nasty," Mi-Mi yelled as they were already gone.

Mi-Mi sat on the other side of the couch and turned the TV on. In the other room, Stacy was blowing Money's socks off. "Ooh shit. Okay, do y'all thing them," Money said as Stacy was deep-throating him. She took him out her mouth and started hooking up and down his shaft down to his balls. She started kissing and licking his balls while she was jacking him off.

Back in the living room, Young Money was tryna get his dick wet, so he went to sit on the other couch where Mi-Mi was sitting. "Wassup, I'm tryna see what that shit do," Young Money said.

"Boy, you aint ready for me. I have yo lil ass sprung." Mi-Mi and Young Money were the same age. She was poppin' it like she had it like that.

"What? I'll break yo lil ass off, you already know, wassup," said Young Money.

"I don't know nothing. You gon' have to show me."

"You ain't saying nothing." Young Money wiped out instantly.

Mi-Mi was just staring at his dick in awe. "Oow okay, I didn't know it was like that. I mean, I heard. I guess they say seeing is believing." And she grabbed Young Money's dick and started massaging his dick, moving it up and down. Once she got him to a full erection, she put him inside her mouth. She started off slow. She only had him halfway in her mouth, but she already had Young Money talking shit to her.

"Damn yo head go crazy." He could have sworn her mouth felt like a wet pussy.

Back in the room, Money was on the verge of bustin' a nut. Stacy peeped how Money was tryna fuck her face, so she let him do his thang. Once Money came, she swallowed every last drop. As Money finished coming, she got him back hard. Once she got him back hard, she got on top of him and started riding him reverse cowgirl style. Now Stacy was bad. She favored Draya Michele from basketball wives of Miami. "Ooh shit, Money. I love this dick. I wonna have yo baby." Stacy's pussy was getting wetter and wetter as she was moving her hips back and forth. "Ooh, Money, I'm fenna come. I'm fenna come. Oooooh huhh owww shit fuck."

"That's what I'm talking 'bout. Get that shit," Money said. Once he said that, Stacy sped up, bringing herself to multiple orgasms. As she did that, Money busted a fat nut inside her. Once they were done, she lay in his arms.

Back in the living room, Money had his pants to his ankles and had Mi-Mi bent over the couch, facedown and ass up. As he was deep-stroking her, her pussy sounded like wet slime in yo hand. "Oooh shit, Young Money, you fenna make me cum!"

"You gon' cum for me. Cum all on this dick for me then."

"Oow, yo dick so good. I swear you dat, nigga."

And she began cumming, legs shaking and everything. Young Money continued pounding her from the back. As he was fenna cum, he slid up out of her and took the condom off and nutted on her ass. Once he got done, he pulled his pants up. Mi-Mi went to the bathroom, cleaned herself up, and walked back to the living room.

Young Money had a wood rolled up. He texted his brother. "Hurry up, lover boy."

"I'm a my way right now. Ayy, did you fuck o girl?"

"Come on, man. You know I did my thang."

"Okay, okay, I taught my son well."

Money came walking out; Stacy walked him to his car. "So is I'ma get to see you again?" Mi-Mi asked Young Money.

"Yea, it's all good. I definitely gotta double back. What's yo number?"

Mi-Mi gave him her number. "You betta call me. I'm not playing wit you. You gon' have me pull up on Oakdale looking for yo ass. It's good I'ma tap in wit you later."

Young Money gave her a hug and grabbed two handfuls of her ass. "You like that."

"Ass back there, you squeezing it for dear life."

"Ha ha, you funny. You know I like that thang. It's soft back there I cunt gone we.

"Well, if you want it, you can have it all to yoself."

"Yea, we gon' see."

"So when you gon' start coming to see me more? I be missing you," Stacy said.

"I mean, now that I got my own whip, I'ma pull up on you."

"Don't be telling me anything. And how you get this car anyway?"

"Oh, you know, I bust a power move. Nothing too much."

"You better be careful, Money. I don't want nothing to happen to you."

"Don't trip. I'ma be good."

"All right, I love you."

"Love you too."

Money and Young Money pulled off on the way back to the projects. They pulled up to the projects and saw Jay shooting dice. "Ayy, Jay nigga, what's popn'?" Money said as he was leaning back in his new whip, smoking on some looks. "Jay, stop shooting dice."

"Okay, I see who getting money when you copped this thang."

"Shit, me and Money just cashed out earlier. Shit I need to go cop me a whip to then yea, you need to end get out that granny car, you crazy. My nigga Venna been getting us everywhere." Venna was the name he gave his Volkswagen.

"What you got going on anyway?" Jay said.

"Shit cooln' me in Money just came from that bitch Stacy's house."

"O yea, her untie was there?"

"Nah, Mi-Mi that ass was over there. For real, I wanted to hit dat shit. I heard she got some good-ass pussy."

"I'm already knowing dat nigga Young Money bent that shit over."

"Wow, dat's crazy. He beat me to it. Where that nigga at anyway?" Jay said.

"You know that nigga somewhere in traffic, but what u fenna get into?"

"Shit, I'm fenna finish taking these niggas' money."

"I'm fenna come get some of dat shit too." Money parked his car and went to the dice game.

* * *

Young Money was slidin' to the neck, smoking on some gilado looking for his next lick. He found himself somewhere in Berlin game that was where all the fat spots were at. As he was slidin' through different neighborhoods, he saw a family of four getting inside of a Bentley truck. "I know they got that bag up in there." He sat low in his car, watching the car pull off. Once he saw they was gone, he pulled off.

That next week, Young Money was ready to bust his move. He had been watching the house for about a week now. He knew that the people who lived in the house were about to hit. They leave every day around 9:30 a.m. and come back at twelve noon, so he knew that he had some room to wiggle. "Look, y'all, this how it's fenna go down," Young Money said as they were sitting in the car parked across the street from the house. This bitch got an alarm in her house, but peep game she think she slick, but I know she don't got no motion sensor on because she got a dog in the house."

"Man, she gotta dog," Money said.

"Yea, scary-ass nigga. She gotta dog, but it's a lil mut. I got some bear mace for dat bitch. So look, I'ma go through the back door, I'ma break the window with a window puncher. That way, we don't trigger the alarm."

"Money, if that lil mut run up, spray his ass. Jay, keep point. Any funny shit pop off, hit me and let me know."

"You know I got chu. You niggas hurry up in do yall shit so we can get the fuck up out of here."

Money and Young Money hopped out the car, looking like some landscapers. They had they tools and all as they headed to the backyard. Young Money took out his window puncher, and the good thing about that was it didn't make no noise; it shattered silently. Once he shattered the glass, he pressed on it lightly, and the back patio window came down.

Like clockwork, once they entered the house, the lil dog came running up barking. Money instantly took out the mace and sprayed the dog. Once he did that, it took off running. Young Money went to work. "Money, you check the downstairs, and I'ma check upstairs."

They both ran through the house like a storm hit it. "Young Money, I found it, bra. Bring yo ass downstairs." He came flying down the stairs.

"What you find, nigga?"

"I found the safe, stupid, where it's at. It's in his office. That bitch heavy. It's gon' take me in you to carry it."

The safe wasn't no bigger than a rolling suitcase. Young Money called Jay to bring the car to the front. As Jay pulled to the front, Money and Young Money were struggling carrying the safe. "Hold up, nigga, 'fore you drop it," Money said.

"Shut up, nigga. I am holding it."

At the sight of the safe, Jay's eyes got wide. Once they finally got the safe in the car, Young Money went to go grab the tools they had left behind. He got the tools, and they drove off. Jay was being hysterical. "Oh shit, you niggas got a fucking safe. How much you think it's in there?" He kept asking question after question.

"Nigga, shut the fuck up in drive. Do it look like we know? We ain't even opened it yet," Young Money said. Once they made it back to the projects, they went to Danyale's house to crack open the safe. "Hold that bitch still," Young Money said to Money as he was trying to crack the safe open with the crowbar. "I almost got it popped." The safe popped open. Young Money couldn't believe his eyes. What he saw made him sick to his stomach. It was a gang of paperwork, three guns, and fifteen thousand in cash. "This some bullshit, bra. I thought we had that bag. This shit ain't nothing."

"Shit, at least it's something. That's a few dollas right there in plus we got some cannons to shit. We get one apiece," Jay said.

"Yea, I hear you." Young Money split the money up; they got $5,000 apiece.

"What ya'll fenna do? I'm about to go put the money up and go bust a few moves," Young Money said.

"Shit, I'm cooln' I'm fenna post up wit baby."

"Jay, what about you?"

"I don't know. Since I'm 5,000 dollas richer, I'm feeln' good. I'm fenna go get some pussy."

"Aight, I'ma tap in wit you niggas later. Oh yea, Money keep the straps over here."

After he said that, Young Money left out the door. "What the fuck is wrong wit that nigga?" Jay said.

"Man, I don't know. You know that nigga siked out he be in his on world."

"Aight then, bra, I'm fenna get up out of here. I got some bunz on deck."

Jay walked to his house. Once he got to his room, he pulled his safe out of his closet. He put the combination in, and the sight he seen once he opened it was a beautiful one. Jay still had all his money from the first lick. He put his money. He just got in some rubber bands and threw it back in the safe. Once he did that, he was tryna figure out what bitch he was fenna go cat off wit. "I know who I'm fenna call. I'm fenna call dat bitch I knocked on the gram, Fendi Bandz."

Ring, ring. "What's good?"

"I don't know, nigga. You tell me."

"Shit cooln' tryna see you."

"O yea, I guess."

"So wassup, I'm fenna come pull up on you."

"Send me yo address."

Fendi sent him the address, and he was on his way. Once he got to her house, he knocked on the door. She opened the door with a tank top in a red thong. Fendi knew what she was doing. She was trying to hypnotize him wit her beauty and looks. She was a sexy caramel. She had a face like Stacey Dash and ass like Melyssa Ford as she walked off and headed to her room. She was walking extra hard, making her ass jiggle from left to right. "Damn, this bitch got hella ass." Jay closed the door and followed Fendi to her room.

"So wassup, Jay? When you gon' take a bitch shopping? I need me a new bag, and I know you getting money. That's the word around the city that you in them other boys you bet wit."

"O yea, that's what they saying. I mean, you know we doing are than, but wassup thow? I'm tryna get some head," Jay said.

Fendi looked at him and smacked her lips. "You tryna see what this neck do, huh? I guess I can give you a lil sample." She took Jay's penis out his pants.

"Oow, I see you workin' wit something."

She started to massage his dick up and down and then she put her mouth on him. Umm slurp slurp as she was going up and down with her mouth on his dick. She turned around and got in a 69 position. Jay was caught off guard. He only ate some pussy like once or twice in his life, and this was gon' be his third time. He slid her red thong to the side and started licking and sucking on her pussy as she still had him in her mouth. "Ooh shit, Jay, yea, just like that. You gon' make me cum." As Fendi was reaching her climax, she got up and got right on top of him and started riding Jay's dick like a female jockey. "Oooh, Jay, this dick feel so good. I want you to bust inside me. Jay, ooh this yo pussy. Jay, tell me this yo pussy." Her pussy was feeling so good Jay was willing to tell her anything to get some more.

"This my pussy," Jay said.

"Oooh yes, it's all yours, Daddy. Oh my god, I'm gonna cum." Fendi sped up rocking back and forth, putting that pussy on him, making sure she gave it to him real good. She wanted him all to herself. She didn't stop riding his dick until he nutted all inside her. Fendi got up and went to go get a hot wet face towel to wipe Jay off.

"Damn, bra, I can't believe I just fucked this bitch raw."

"You good? You look lost in space."

"Yea, I'm good. I was just thinking how good that pussy was feelin'."

"Oh yea, I got that good good. Once Fendi put this pussy on you, you gon' keep coming back like a junkie who need they fix."

"Yea, I hear you, so when I'ma get to see you again?"

"Whenever you want this yo pussy, whenever you want it," she said after giving him a wet kiss on the lips.

"Aight, well, I'ma fenna go bust a few moves I'ma tap in with you later."

"You betta call me, boy." Jay left and got in traffic.

Young Money was sliding around smoking, thinking about today's festivities. "I can't believe this shit. That heavy-ass safe only had fifteen punk-ass thousand. I gotta do better. I'm tryna get that pany. Only time will tell." His phone rang, breaking him from his thoughts.

"Wassup, stranger?" Mulan said. "Where you been? Haven't heard from you in a while."

"Shit, I've been busy."

"Busy doing what?"

"Getting to this bag."

"Is that right? Get that money then. Well, I was just calling to see what you was doing. I was thinking bout you."

"You was thinking 'bout the kid. Let me know it's real then. Where you at anyway?"

"At home. Why? You gon' come see."

"Yea, I'ma pull up on you in a min."

"Yea, we a see." Young Money got off the phone. He was tryna be inside something to relieve some tension, and he knew he wasn't fenna fuck Mulan no time soon. He knew the perfect candidate. Ring, ring. TaTa picked up her phone ASAP.

"Wassup wit TaTa?"

"Nigga, don't wassup TaTa. Me you phony is fucy, my nigga. You ain't been picking yo phone up for me or nothing like that. You got me fucked up for real. Niggas get money in act like they don't know nobody, in to top it off, I haven't even been inside that car you just bought."

"Is you done yet?"

"No, I'm not. I can go on in on. Shall I say more?"

"No, say less? Wassup though? I'm fenna come get you. Be outside yo house in five minutes."

"Yea, whatever."

Ta was juiced that Young Money was coming to get her in. Since she fired all her side niggas, she haven't had no dick since the last time they fucked. Young Money pulled up outside of TaTa's house. Honk, honk. "Damn, why you gotta rush a bitch?"

"Gone with that shit. Roll this up." He threw her some woods and a quarter of cooks. As she was rolling up the woods, she seen somebody tryna FaceTime him. She wasn't gon' say nothing; she didn't wanna ruin the moment. Young Money slid to Twin Peaks. It was a lil spot everybody went to. It was a tourist attraction site. It was on top of a hill overlooking the whole city

"Young Money, I missed you, baby. I haven't seen you in forever. I like yo car. What bitch you had in here? Let me find out you had a bitch up in here. I'ma beat that hoe ass."

Young Money was puffing on his wood, not even listening to what she was saying. He really was tryna get his dick sucked. "Come here real quick."

"What you want, Young Money?" TaTa had her lips Mac up lip gloss poppin' as she said that.

"Man, you know what I want. I'm tryna get some of that top you got."

"Is you? You want me to put my mouth on yo dick?"

"Yea, I do."

And then he unbuttoned his pants. TaTa leaned over and grabbed Young Money's dick out his pants. "Oooh, I missed this dick," she said as she was putting kisses all around his dick. Young Money loved the way she gave him head. As she put him in her mouth, she had her rhythm down pack. She started off slow, then she started deep-throating him, putting him to the back of her throat. She did anything to please him. She did that several times. She didn't want to make him come yet. "Young Money, I wants some dick," she said in a lil whining voice. They hopped in the back seat, and they both got undressed. Young Money started sucking on her titties, one titty at a time. Once he got done, he slid inside her; she was so tight and wet. Young Money found his rhythm and started beating her pussy up. "Oooh, Young Money, I love this dick so much." She had her legs locked around his waist as he was dicking her down.

"Who pussy is this?"

"Oooh, this yo pussy. I swear this yo pussy. It's all yours, baby. Ooh yes, keep fucking me like that. I'ma bout to come. Ooh, oh my god. I'm coming." As she was coming, Young Money kept fucking her and nutted inside her. "Wooh, that shit was everything," TaTa said as she was putting her clothes on. "Young Money, you know I love you so much."

"I got love for you too."

He started his car up and drove off. He dropped her off and went home to go wash up. Once he got done getting dressed, he headed to Mulan's house. Ring, ring. "Hello, Mulan," he said in a sleepy voice. "Open the door. I'm outside." Mulan came to the door in her bra and panties and looking sexy as fuck with her headscarf on.

"Took you long enough. I fucked around and fell asleep on yo ass."

"My bad, I had to handle some business."

"Yea, I hear you." Mulan went to her drawer to put on a shirt. "So what do I owe you for this visit?"

"Man, you play too much." Young Money grabbed the remote and turned on the TV. Once he did that, he broke down a wood and rolled up some cookies. "How was yo day?" Young Money asked Mulan.

"It was cool. Long is fuck. I show a be happy once I'm finished wit this semester, then I would have one more semester left till I graduate. Man, I can't wait. How 'bout you? How was your day?"

"I can't call it. Tryna get this money, get to a bag fill me." He inhaled the weed smoke after he said that.

"And what is it that you actually do to get this bag you say you tryna get?"

"It's complicated. I don't wanna scare you off."

"Scare who? Me? Boy, stop playing. You must I me. I'm definitely wit the shit."

"O yea, is that right? Since you put it like that, I'ma keep it all the way a hunned wit you."

"Please do."

"I be breaking into houses and taking people's money in jewelry. That's wassup. Let me hit that blunt."

Mulan took a few puffs to get her mind right because what she was fenna tell him was gon' change the events in their lives. "I gotta tell you something." She took Young Money out of his thoughts.

"What? You finally gon' give me some pussy?" he said wit a smile on his face.

"Uhh, no, you ain't getting none of that yet, not til you show me it's real. And anyway, you gon' know when I'm ready, but like I was fenna say, I gota way you can get some money." Once she said that, she had his full attention.

"Speak on it. I'm listening."

"All right, look, I got some people who you can get. My aunties and uncles on my mom side of the family own all types of business, and they keep their money at they house. All you gotta do is go there when they gone, and you a be good."

"Let me ask you something. Why yo folks though?"

"Because them bitches never fucked wit me and my mom, so fuck 'em."

"Is you wit it or not?"

"Fuck yea I'm with it. I'm TTG trained to go. Let me know when you ready, in I'ma but my move. Yep, it's good. Give me like a week, in I'ma be ready," Mulan said.

Young Money was so ready to hit the lick he could barely sleep. He went over everything wit Mulan the day before. "Okay, Young Money. Look, my uncle and auntie own a illegal gambling shack Fri through Sat, and they go to church on Sunday at 8:45 a.m., and they don't get back until sometime in the afternoon. That should give you enough time to bust ya'll move. Now I don't know where they keep the money, but I do know they don't believe in bank accounts, so the money in there. You just gotta look for it."

"Don't even trip. I got it. I'ma make it happen," Young Money said.

The following weekend, they was ready, and everybody knew their position. "Look, Jay," said Young Money, "make shore you on point. You see any bing bings walking this way, call me and let me know."

"My nigga, how many times you gotta tell me? I know what I'm doing. I got this."

"Aight, come on, Money. Let's go get paid."

As they was walking up toward the house, Young Money peeped; it wasn't no alarm. He whispered to Money, "Ayyy, bra, it ain't no alarm on this bitch. We definitely in this thang." As he put the crowbar inside the door and tugged on it a few times, it popped open. "Come on, bra. We in here." Once they got in this house, they searched high and low.

"Damn, bra, where the fuck the money at?" Money said. "I thought you said it was in here. You brought us on this bogus-ass mission."

"Shut up, my nigga. It's in here, I'm telln you. Keep looking."

Young Money went to go look in the garage. As he was looking through shit, he seen a deep freezer and went to go open it. He seen hella fresh fish. He was about to close it. "Fuck it, let me check this shit."

Once he emptied all the fish out, it was stacks of hunnids, fittys, and twenties. "Ayy, Money," he screamed, "bring yo ass here."

Wassup? You betta had . . . oh shit, look at all that money."

"I told yo scrub ass it was in here to get some pillowcases."

Once they grabbed the money, they headed out the house and got in the car. Jay drove off. "Damn, my nigga, why the fuck ya'll smell like some dead pussy?"

"All, man, you know a nigga had to get dirty for that money," Young Money said. "Ayy, Jay, watch when you see how much money we got in the bag."

"Shit, fuck, waitn' let me see that shit right now."

Young Money opened the pillow case. "Oh shit, my nigga, how much money is that?"

"Shit, I don't even know. We feena find out once we get to the spot."

Once they made it to Danyale's spot, Jay bagged the car in the parking stall, and they got out and went in the house. "Ayy, Young Money, bra, no holla though. You stank like fuck. You mind as well hop in the shower real quick. I gotta brand-new Nike sweat suit you can put on and some boxer briefs in all that good shit you need."

"Aight, I'm fenna go hop in the shower. You pussy bet not touch nothing while I'm gone."

"The fuck this nigga think he is? We fenna count up, grab some of that money."

Once Jay and Money started counting, Young Money was walking back to the living room. "What you hopped in and out that, mafucka?" Jay said.

"Yea, I did. I knew you niggas was gon' start counting wit'out a nigga. What it's looking like?"

"Shit, we already at $50,000, and we still got them stacks right there," Money said.

"Okay, datts wassup," Young Money said wit a smile on his face. He joined the group and started counting. Once they got done, the count came up to $150,000. Once they figured out how much money they had, they was juiced. "Nigga, we eatn'. I gotta put this shit on the gram. We fenna go live." Jay and Money was wit it. They all grabbed some stacks and way flexin' and talking big shit. "Yea, man, we gettn' to that bag. You see it whole team eatin', you broke niggas. Catch up."

"Ayy, Money, you go that bag on you." Young Money was filming him off his iPhone. Ayy, look, you know I got that bag on me. Ya heard mi. Ayy, you niggas betta cuff yo bitch because if she slide in my din, I'ma fuck da shit out of her straight up. Ayy, Jay bandz, how you fuck wit it, you know?"

"You know, getting to it." As he said that, he was thumbing through all the money. "And there you have it, whole team movin' mean straight up. Ayyy, we was just going up on da gram. Ma'fuckas know what it is. Watch when I get that panning them bitches gon' be on my dick. Wassup, you niggas tryna go to the mall. We got all this money. Let's go get fresh," Jay said.

"Sounds like a plan to me," Money said. "I'm wit it." Once they got done shopping, they had name brands that consisted of Jordans, Phocum Possit Supreme, Bape in Ape, Balmain, Gucci, and Louis Vuitton. Once they got back, they all went their separate ways.

I hope everything went smooth, Mulan was thinking to herself. She didn't hear from Young Money all day. She was wondering what was taking him so long to call her. Ring, ring. Speaking of the devil. She answered the phone going 90 North. "Oh my god, is everything all right with is you? Okay where you at?"

"Chill out. I'm good. Take a deep breath."

Mulan took a sigh of relief. "So did everything so good."

"Yea, everything went smooth. Matter of fact, I'm on my way to yo house right now. I talk to you more about it once I get there."

"Okay, I see you when you get here."

Young Money pulled up to her house and walked towards the house. Before he could even walk in, Mulan already was at the door looking all nervous and shit. "Hurry up in come in."

"First off, why is you whispering? Second of all, why is you acting all nervous? I told you everything good," as Young Money came in. She shut the door and locked it. After she did that, she started looking through the blinds. You siked out for real, you doing hella shit right now. Bring yo ass over here in chill out."

Once she sat down, Young Money rolled up some cooks he fired up, took a few hits, and passed Mulan the blunt. After she took a few puffs and started coughing. "Woola, I needed that. My nerves was driving me through the roof and yo big head," as she grabbed the pillow and playfully hit him with it. "You had me worried. Why you didn't call me when everything got done?"

"I don't know. Me in my niggas went to the mall and went shopping."

"Did you get me something?"

"Nah, I got something better than clothes, and what's better than that?" Young Money reached in his pants pocket and tossed her a stack of money.

"O my god, Young Money, how much money is this?"

"I don't know. Want you count it in see."

Mulan took the rubber band off and started counting. As she was doing that, Young Money was enjoying the back wood he had rolled up. "This is $7,500. What am I'm gon' do with all this money?"

"Shit, whatever you want to do with it."

"Okay, but let me ask you something. How much did y'all come up with?"

"Shit we hit fa like $150,000." Mulan couldn't believe her ears. She knew the other side of her family was getting money but not like that. She got on top of Young Money and straddled him. Once she did that, she started kissing him. Now you know she shushed him. As she continued to kiss, him she laid him down on the couch. She lifted his shirt up and started putting kisses all over his chess and his stomach. She kept going lower and lower. Once she reached his Gucci belt, she unbuckled it and pulled his dick out. She was satisfied of the sight she was looking at in her hand. She started to massage his dick up and down in her hand. Once she got him to reach a full erection, she was just staring at his penis. "I can't believe I'm about to do this." She put her mouth around him and began to move her head up and down. Once she went down, she scraped the tip of his dick wit her teeth.

"Amm, wait. Look, babe, this is not a Snicker. Act like you sucking on a popsicle."

"Okay, popsicle, got it." Once she got back at it, she only used her lips and her tongue. As she had her rhythm going, Young Money grabbed her head and guided her.

"Oh shit! Damn, my nigga, that shit feel hella good." It seemed like once he said that, he busted a fat nut in her mouth. Mulan ran to the bathroom and spitted it in the toilet and washed her mouth out with mouthwash.

"You so nasty. Why you didn't tell me you was cumming?"

"Man, I don't know. That shit was feelin too good."

"Oh yea, I low-key knew what I was doing. That's crazy. That was my first time."

"I could tell. You damn near bit my shit off. What made you go all in like that?"

"I don't know. I was just feelin it."

"Okay, I feel special," Young Money said.

"Well, you should cuz you the only one I did that too."

"Aww, come here, baby." He grabbed her, and she laid on his chest.

The summer was almost over, and Young Money was at the peak of his game. He copped that Porsche Panamera he wanted; he also copped a bust-down Rolly in Cuban, and not to mention, he had $200,000 put up. Money and Jay also copped some foreign whips plus the jewelry to go with it, and like Young Money, they also had $200,000 put up. "Man, bra, it's been a good summer," Jay said as all three of them were on a sandy white beach, leaning back in some beach chairs on Miami Beach.

"You ain't never lied. We definitely in a bag. Wassup wit you, Young Money? Why you so quiet?" Money asked him.

"Shit, I'm just thinking we been getting money all summer, and I know I said we was gon' only fuck around for the summer, and right now, I feel like we should keep it lit."

"The fuck you mean keep it lit? Its bad enuff we done took penitentiary chances, you act like we ain't got no money put up," Money said.

"Yea, we got money put up, but how long you think that money gon' last, give or take another year? Then what? Back to the basics. Fuck nah, not me. I'm gon' get to this bag."

"What bout you, Jay? You still tryna get to this bag?"

"Hell yea, you know I'm wit it. You need to talk to yo boy cause he's on some bullshit," Young Money said. Money walked off down the beach deep in thought.

* * *

Later that night, all three of them was turning up at KOD, King of Diamonds. It was bad bitches all around them. They had bottles of d'usse, and ace of spade covered the table. Everybody was on they level as a big booty freak was shaking her ass for Young Money. Money put his arm around Young Money and took a swig of the ace of spade he was drinking. "Check it out," he said over the loud music that was playing. "You my mafuckn' brotha, you hear me."

"Yea, I hear you." Young Money was throwing ones on the striper. As he was talking, he knew Money was drunk.

"You my twin, my nigga, so if you still want to get this money, I'm all in. I got yo right, left, and front. Fill me, yea, I fill you now. That's what the fuck I'm talking 'bout. I need you, my nigga. I can't trust nobody else besides you in Jay. Matter of fact, where dat nigga at anyway."

"You know dat nigga's on his freaky shit. He went to one OC, then back rooms wit a bad bitch I could of swearn it was Blac Chyna," Money said.

"Nigga, Blac Chyna don't even strip no more," Young Money said, laughing.

"O yea, huh, I must be swerun."

"I'm fenna see who I'm fenna take back there. I'm holla at you in a few."

Young Money rolled up a wood and sat back and enjoyed the show. In front of him were two yellow bones shaking they ass. Young Money thought to himself, *This definitely living.* After the club, they all left with some bunz, and they all got some pussy that night and got ready for they flight the next day.

"Home sweet home," Jay said as the plane landed.

"Ayy, we had a hell of summer. We ran it up, got foreign whips bust down. Jewelry in all lat," Young Money said.

"We still got hella plays up, so we fenna get back to it. Is your niggas ready to get back to this, Money."

"Fuck yea, Jay in," Money said.

Once they got back to the city, everybody went their separate ways. Young Money hopped in his panny and bent a few corners. As he was driving, he seen the gang task force get behind. "Fuck those bitch-ass faggots, always fucking with a nigga." Young Money pulled over. Once he did that, Officer Robbert and two of his flunkies hopped out of the car and approached the vehicle.

"Hahh, what's going on, Mr. Young Money? Nice car. You gotta better car than me."

"All man, you know it bee like that."

"O, do it? See look it here. I'ma be straightforward with you. It's been a lot of break-ins throughout San Francisco."

"Okay, the fuck that got to do wit me?"

"It got a lot to do with you, motherfucker," said one of the flunkies.

"Chill out," said Officer Robbert. "I got this. Now look, Young Money, I don't care if you break into people houses. Just don't break in to none out here."

"Man, I don't know what the fuck you talking 'bout? Matter of fact, em I under arrest?"

"No, you're not."

"Aight, is you done because I'm done having this conversation wit you?"

"Yea, I'm done. Just know I'm watching you."

"Yea, I hear." After he said that, Young Money turned his music up and blasted off. "Bitch ass 12 can't fuck wit me," he said to hisself. Ring, ring.

"Hello," Mi-Mi said, "wassup wit you? What you got going on?"

"Nothin, chillen' wit my right hand. Wassup wit chu? Where you been at stranger?"

"Shit getting to this bag fill me."

"I heard."

"What's good though? You gon' come see me. Yea, I'm fenna pull up on you."

"All right, I'ma see you when you get here." He hung up and headed to Mac-block.

Ring, ring, "Ayy, I'm outside."

"All right, I'm fenna come out right now." Once Mi-Mi was walking towards the car, she said to herself, "Oow, this nigga got a Porsche. I gotta get fucked in this whip. Wassup wit Young Money? I like you car. When you get this one?"

"Shit, like a few weeks ago."

"Look at you. You think you dat niggas think."

"Nah, I don't think I know."

"Yea, yea, I hear. Wassup? Can we go somewhere? I'm bored of being in the house."

"Where you tryna go?"

"Anywhere. I'm just tryna be around you. I been missing you since that last time we fucked."

"Is that right?"

"Yea, that's all the way right. I told you, you fenna be my nigga." Young Money pulled off, busted a few laps through the Moe, and went uptown to the Philly Cheese Steak spot on Divisadero. Once they finished eating, Money was on his way to drop Mi-Mi off, but as he was driving, she undid his Hermes belt, unzipped his pants, and put his dick right in her mouth. She started deep-throating him of da dribble. Her head game was so vicious he had to pull over on a side street. As she continued to slobber him down, she took him all the way to the back of her throat that caused her to choke in gag.

"Ooh, Young Money, I love sucking yo dick."

"Umm huh, suck it just like that." As he grabbed her head, she spread up, and he pushed her head all the way down on his dick. As he came in her mouth, she swallowed every drop.

"Uhmm, that tasted good," Mi-Mi said. Young Money started up his car to go drop her off. Once he pulled up, she tried to give Young Money a kiss. He turned his cheek to her, and she kissed his cheek. "So when I'ma get to see y'all again?" She was referring to him and his dick.

"I mean, shit if you said it like that, I'ma tap back in wit you ASAP."

"Yea, you need to cause I need my issue. I want some dick."

"Don't trip. I got you. I'ma pull up on you in a few."

"You betta. I'm not playin wit you. I'm really fillen' everything about you. I guess it's something 'bout you dat I crave."

"O yea, it's something that I crave about you too."

"And what's that?"

"Yo mouth," he said and chuckled. "But nah, for real, you cool. I'm diggn' yo style."

"Aight, I'm feelin what you sayn. Call me, aight? I'ma hit you in a few." Young Money pulled off.

It was a week until Mulan's birthday. She was indecisive on what she wanted to do. "Bitch, you playn. We mind as well piece up on a suite at the MGM. You can invite yo lil boo. He can bring my nigga, and Chanele can hop on Money, and we can get them to get us a table in some bottle service," Fendi said.

"Bitch, I don't need him to do nothing. I got my on money. I can get my own table."

"But Vegas do sound fun."

"So is we gon' turn up what because you tryna be on some basic shit bitch? You fenna be twenty-one. We gotta be all the way live," Chanele said.

"I mean, we can hit Vegas," Mulan said.

"O yea, we fenna be lit. We gon' turn you up, cuzz," Fendi said. "First thing first, we gotta go shopping."

"But the malls out here really don't be having nothing," Mulan said.

"Bitch, we fenna go to Saks Fifth in the city on Union Square. They be having everything up in there. We need to get on it because lil Ms. Thang be taking forever to pick her outfits," Chanele said.

"Well, let's get dressed so we can get up out of here in go get cute."

"That's crazy. You really fenna be twenty-one. Aww, my baby cuzn gettn grown out here. Now you don't gotta be asking me to use my ID," Fendi said. "So, cuz, is you gon' give dat pussy to Young Money or nah. I don't know why you keep teasing dat boy, and he getting money. You betta stop playing 'fore somebody snatch him up."

"Girl, I ain't worried about none of that. He know wassup in why y'all all in my business. This is my pussy. I'ma give it to whoever I feel that's worthy," Mulan said wit a smile on her face.

"Girl, you know you fenna give dat pussy to Young Money. I don't know why you even frontin'," Chanele said.

"Is you bitches ready?" Fendi was ready to go shopping. Jay gave her a few dolls, and she was tryna go spend every dollar.

"Shit, we was waiting on yo ass. You know you be taking forever in a day to get ready," Mulan said.

"You bitches, don't be hatin. You know I gotta be on point when I step out."

"Yea, dat part."

Once they got to Saks Fifth, they all went their separate way. Each one of them was tryna outdo the next, but when it came down to it, Mulan had the best dress hands down. She had purchased a YSL Yves Saint Laurent dress. It was a strapless all black, and it barely covered up her ass.

"Oow, bitch, I'm hella mad. I wanted to get that dress, but they didn't have it in my size," Fendi said. "I ain't gon' lie, you killin them in dat dress. You gon' be fuckn' them up."

"I do like it," Mulan said as she was looking in the dressing room mirror.

Ring, ring, ring. "Wassup wit you?" Young Money said over FaceTime.

"You see, me getn' this dress for my b-day."

"Let me see what that shit looking like." She turned the iPhone to the left and right. "Okay, I see you. Somebody gon' be killin' 'em."

"Boy, we all gon' be killen' 'em."

"Fuck you talkn' 'bout?" Fendi said after she took the phone from Mulan. Mulan kept sizen' her dress up. "Wassup wit my sister?"

"Oh, I'm yo sister now."

"Yea, you sister."

"You so phony."

"Wassup wit you in my brother Jay?"

"Datt nigga know wassup. Dats my nigga straight up. Ayy, though, I know you betta come through for my best friend."

"Ayy, you know I'm ready on dat."

"Yea, we gon' see." She handed the phone back to Mulan.

"Ayy, babe, what time are movie start?" Mulan said.

"Like at ten p.m."

"Okay, so don't be late. You know how you be in dice games in shit act like you got ambisig. Man, I'ma pull up. Ayy, babe, I'ma hit you in a minute I'm fenna get in traffic."

* * *

Young Money slid to go get his car washed on Protreo Street. As he was sitn' in the waitin' area, he seen some older niggas that Shota was beefn' wit. He knew that was them because he remember that car from riding.

"Oooh, Jay, you bout to make me cum. Yes, keep fucking me like that," Fendi said as Jay had her facedown, ass up. He was getting straight back shots. Fendi was throwing that ass back on 'em like her life depended on it. After a few rounds, they both were winded. "So is you coming to Vegas with us for my cuzn b-day?" Fendi had asked Jay as she was lying on his chess with her leg laying across his.

"Yea, I'm coming. You know we fenna act up we gon' be on are bougie. You know how me in my niggas do."

"Yea, I heard. Let me see any bitch tryna be in yo face, I'ma beat that bitch ass."

"Why you wanna do all that?" he said as he was rubbing on her booty.

"I'm just saying don't get to Vegas and be acting brand-new like you don't know wassup."

"I mean, I think you gon' have to remind me."

"Boy, don't play out wit me. I'ma remind you, all right." She started to massage his dick up and down and put him inside her mouth. As she begun deep-thoatn him, Jay grabbed her head and started fucking her mouth. Fendi was lovn' every bit of it. She didn't want Jay to come yet, so she got on top of him and started riding his dick. "Umm, huh, this dick so good. Who dick is this?" Fendi said.

"This yo shit," Jay answered.

"Ooh, you bet not give this dick to nobody, I swear, huhha. Ooh fuck, I'm fenna come." As she was coming, she sped her rhythm up, coming all over Jays dick. Once she did that, he busted a fat nut inside her. Fendi sat there for several minutes; she was still climaxing as Jay was still inside her. She got up and went to the bathroom to go get a wet face towel to wipe Jay off. "You hungry?" Fendi asked him.

"Hell yea, I'm hungry. What you gon' cook?"

"What you want to eat?"

"Shit, since you said it like that, I want some steak, a baked potato, some prawns, and some garlic bread and some asparagus."

"Damn greedy-ass lil boy. You gon' eat a bitch out a house in a home, but I got you, babe."

As she went to go cook his food, he turned the 49ers game on and leaned back on the bead with both his hands behind his head. "This is liven'."

In the car with Shota, he FaceTimed 'em. What's popn'? Ayy, cuzz, why dem suckas right here playn?"

"Who?"

"Dem Garliton niggas."

"Ayy you got yo blower on you?" Shota asked.

Young Money said, "Hell yeah, you know I got dat xd glock 27 on me wit the hockey stick on it."

"Look at my young boy on his shit dem niggas. Can't see you."

"Nah, I'm right here by the taco stand."

"Aight, look, keep yo hand on yo strap. Any funny shit, air dem niggas out and get up out of there."

"Most definitely." Once Money got off the phone, his car was ready. He pushed past them as he was watching all three of them. After he got in his Panamera, he blasted off.

"Man bet one hundred shoot a hunned," the boy on the dice said to Money.

"Nigga, you betta stop acting like you ain't getn' money, bet $300."

"Aight, bet."

As the person was shooting the dice, Young Money came flying down the block. "Man, this nigga wild," Money whispered to hisself.

"Wassup, Money?" Young Money said as he pulled up, hanging out the window.

"Shit, you see me tryna get a few dollas."

"O yea, I see you were dat nigga Jay at shit I don't know somewhere around here."

"So look, bra, my bitch b-day coming up next week. She going to Vegas. Y'all niggas tryna come."

"Fuck yea. You know I'm pullen' up. When we leaving?"

"Shit we gon' leave on the seventh of November."

"Aight."

"I'm fenna go to the house. I'ma tap in wit you in a minute."

"Aight, bra, I'm 'bout to finish taking these niggas' money." Young Money pulled off and went to the house. Once he made it home, his phone rung. He seen who it was and sent her to the voice mail. He didn't feel like being bothered. Only thing that was on his mind was getting some money and his babe Mulan. He sat back on his bed and broke down a back wood and rolled up some cookies. After he finished rolling up the blunt, he turned on the 49ers game and zoned out

"Come on, babe. Hurry up. The movie fenna start," Mulan said.

"I'm coming. I mean, you the one wonna order everything at the concession stand."

"Don't do me, dude. You know I need my snacks."

As they were watching the movie, Young Money's phone rung. He hit the side button on his iPhone. Mulan peeped what he did and kept her comments to herself for now. Once the movie was over, they headed to his car. "I really enjoyed myself," Mulan said.

"I did too. I really like spending time wit you."

"Aww, you do you. Prolly just telln' me anything."

"Nah, for real, I like are lil vibe we got."

"Yea, we do be chillin," Mulan said.

On the way to her house, Mulan put on Brandy's "The Boy Is Mine." She was singing along with the song and everything. Young Money was just looking at her, smiling. Once he pulled up to her house, he parked his car. "Ayy, let me ask you something," Young Money said.

"Wassup, you really feelin' me?"

"I mean, you cool. I like are lil chemistry we got in all lat, but I see you not really ready to be in a committed relationship and how you figure that."

"Because for one, you think you hella slick. I be on to everything you doing like when one of them bitches call yo phone, you hit the side button on yo phone. Or when a bitch FaceTiming you, you turn yo phone off. Shall I go on?"

"Nah, you good. I mean, you got me on that."

"Yea, I know I do, so stop playing wit me. You gon' fuck around and fuck up the surprise I got for you."

"And what's that?"

"You gon' see if you make it."

"Oh yeah, well, I'm definitely gon' make if you already know wassup. You all me."

"Well, you need to start acting like if you betta let them bitches know what it is."

"Don't trip. I got you," he said with a light grin on his face.

"You think everything funny wit yo big head ass."

"Come here give me a kiss." Young Money leaned over and gave her a peck on the lips.

"Un huh, stop playin' wit me. Give me a real kiss." She grabbed Young Money by the face, and they tongued each other down. They finally broke away from each other. "Damn, boy, you tryna suck my lips off."

"If you only knew."

"Uh, bye, lil nasty. Call me when you make it in."

"Aight, I'ma hit you."

Once Mulan got out the car, Young Money pulled off. He took his phone off silent. It instantly started ringing. "Hello."

"Damn, my nigga. Let me find out you had yo face in Mulan pussy this whole time."

"Nah, bra, I wish. I ain't even got to fuck yet."

"What? That's crazy. You been talking to baby girl for almost six months."

"I know. Tell me about it.

"Her cuzn a freak," Jay said. "I be fuckn' the shit out of her."

"O yea, wassup though. Why the fuck you blown up my phone anyway, nigga?"

"Blood let me tell you why when I was coming out of Fendi spot. You know she stay in the east over them in the dubs. Tell me why when I was bendn' a few corners I seen a fat spot we can hit in the Oakland Hills."

"Aight, you think its sweet though."

"Fuck yea, nigga. Sweet as Mulan pussy."

Young Money laughed. "Watch yo mouth. That's baby, nigga."

"Yea, nigga, whatever. That ain't gon' be baby till you stick yo dick in her."

"Man, dat part, huh."

"But look though," Jay said. "Let's hit that bitch next week before we go to Vegas."

"Oh, so you coming wit us."

"Ayy, you know I'm pulling up."

"Aight, it's all good. Next wIe gettin' to it. This bet not be no bunk mission."

"Man, I got this pa fuck you mean."

"Yea, aight, nigga. Kick rocks." Young Money hung up the phone and headed home.

"You niggas ready to get this money?" Jay said as they pulled up to the spot.

"Damn, this a big-ass house," Young Money said.

"I told you I knew what I was talking 'bout."

"I know, but check it out. This bitch gotta alarm on it. So look, Money, we gang straight to the master room, grab what we can grab, in we out of there in lest in a minute in a half. The police got five minutes to get the call from ADT, so we good."

Young Money and Money approached the house. They knew nobody was there from the information Jay gave them. Young Money took the crowbar out of his sweatpants and wiggled it inside the door. A few tugs he was in. Once he broke inside, the alarm went off instantly. They broke straight upstairs. It seemed like forever getting up the stairs as they got to the master room. They flipped over the mattress, opened drawers, and they stumbled on a jewelry box inside the walk-in closet. "Come on. We gone," Young Money said. They ran out the house and got in the car. Jay pulled off smooth. "My nigga, look all this jewlry," Young Money said as he was pulling the jewelry out the jewelry box.

"Okay, we got bust down everything. Look at all these diamonds," Money'said."

"Dat's what the fuck I'm talking 'bout." Jay banged on the steering wheel.

"Damn, my nigga, don't kill us. You banging all on the steern' wheel in shit."

"Shut up, scary-ass nigga. I got this. I know what I'm doing."

"Yea, aight, nigga. Make shore we make it to the spot," Money said.

Once they got to the spot, they separated the jewelry. "Look at this rowley. This mufucka phat," Young Money said.

"Yea, its fat all right. Don't be getting too comfortable with that rowley. We selling all this shit," Jay said. They had two rowleys, a bust-down one and a plain Jane, a diamond necklace, and a few diamond rings.

"Ayy, I be right back. I'm fenna go meet up wit Shota in see how much this shit hittn foe."

"Oh, animated-ass nigga, you just had to keep the rowley on," said Jay.

"Ayy, this rowley fit my wrist like it was made for it." He recited a verse from YFN Lucci as he was walking out the door. Once he got in the car, he called Shota. Ring, ring. "Wassup, big cuz? What's good?"

"Shit in traffic lookin' for it."

"O yea, I see you tryna get to that bag."

"Already you know I stay on it. What's the deal? What you got going on?"

"All, man, you know we did one thing all bust down, you hear me."

"Okay, okay, I see you. Lil niggas ain't doing no letting up."

"Fuck nah, we getting to it, but look, I'm fenna come drop this off to you. Where you want to meet at?"

"Shit, I'm on my way to the hood right now."

"Aight, shit, you can just meet me at the house."

"Bet I'ma see you in a few."

Once Money got to the house, he went to go take a catnap. Ring, ring. "Open the door, nigga."

"Damn, my nigga, I just closed my eyes."

"Well, nigga, rise in shine. It's money time."

Young Money got up and opened the door for Shota. "Where the shit at?"

"Hold on. Let me go grab it real quick."

As he was grabbing the jewelry, Shota was breaking down a back wood. Rolling up some cookies. "Let me see dat shit, my nigga," Shota said as he inhaled the cookie smoke. "Okay, now this what the fuck I'm talking bout."

"That shit phat, huh," Young Money said.

"Yea, you niggas did yall thang."

"Come on, man. That's all rocky right there. We getn that bag right there. Ayy, let me hit that wood real quick, my nigga," Young Money said. As he took two hits from the wood, Mulan FaceTimed him. "Wassup, babe."

"What you doing, big head?"

"O, you know me, getn' to that bag fill me. You know how I do. In how you do." Money flipped the camera and showed her the jewelry.

"I see somebody in their bag. Okay, you get brown pants for that."

"Yea, man, Christmas came early this year."

"My nigga, when Christmas come past the wood, dude, you over there wit all the extra shit." Young Money hit it three more times, then passed it. "Ayy, babe, you know we fenna be going up in Vegas straight up.

"Yea, we gon' see how you flex. Oh ye, I know about that bitch TaTa."

"O yea, what you telln' me for."

"I see you got jokes, so let me ask you this. Who you rockn' with? You already know you all me ain't no body fucking wit you."

"Yea, aight, you betta control yo lil bitches, for I have too pull up. I know dat bitch from Oakdale."

"Man gone with dat shit."

"But I'ma let you breathe. I was just calling you cuzz I was thinking 'bout you."

"Aight, I'ma pullup on you when I'm done finishing wit this shit."

Young Money hung up the phone. "You ready to get this money?"

"Fuck yea," Young Money said.

"Aight, look I'm fenna holla at my boy. I'm double back later on. I'ma hit you with the score when I see how much is worth."

"Yea, get at me. I'm fenna post up right here."

Shota put the jewelry in the Louis backpack. "Aight, my nigga, tap in," Young Money said. Once Shota left, Young Money went to his room, turned on his TV, and was watching ESPN. He was just sitn' there chillen' in his own thoughts, and he decided to count his money. So he went to his floor safe in his closet. Once he put his combination in, he started grabbing money loafs, and putting them on the bed, he took off the rubber band, and he started counting his money. He did that to several different loafs. After he finished counting, he had a fat grin on his face. His total amount came out to $25,000. He couldn't believe he had all that much now. He knew he had been stacking, but he never had a chance to really count his money." After he finished putting knew rubber bands on his doe, he put his money back in the safe. "Hugh, let me call this bitch." As Young Money leaned back, he FaceTimed TaTa. "What's the deal, my nigga?"

"I don't know, you tell me."

"Shit, a nigga tryna rub on yo booty low-key."

"Yea, miss me wit all lat. You ain't rubbing shit my nigga straight up."

"Why you actn all funny in shit?"

"Cuz I'm mad at you. You some otha you be actn' phony is fuck."

"Man, fuck all lat. Where you at, my nigga?"

"I'm in my skin. That's where I'm at, ain't like you worried."

"I do be worried about you, lil baby."

"Yea, I couldn't tell. Don't you got you a lil girlfriend."

"I don't know but all lat."

"Boy, stop lyn'. I heard you was talking to some bitch from the town, her name Mulan."

"Yea, nigga, I know 'bout all that."

"O yea, I know I'm tryna get some head, so wat's poppn'."

"Ooh, I can't fucking stand yo lil ugly ass."

"Bitch, you know you my lil down ass bitch."

"Ayy, forreal though, pull up up in bring me some weed."

"Aight, I'm fenna be on my way."

As he was waiting for TaTa, he texted Mi-Mi. "Wassup, stranger."

"Nah, you the stranger."

"Dats crazy."

"Yea, I know which one of yo bitches fenna have a b-day party."

Damn, how the fuck all these bitches know about babe? he thought.

"Oh yea, shit yo guess is as good as mine."

"Yea, okay, let me find out. Wassup, though, I miss you."

Right before he was fenna text back, TaTa came knocking at the door. "Open the door, baby daddy."

"Man gone wit that shit."

"Boy, I was just playing. Don't nobody want know baby by yo lil ugly."

"You know wassup. You know I look good."

"Yea, you do look good. Let me suck yo dick right here, man, you siked out."

"You know I'm over you, baby."

As she said that, she walked off. Young Money was staring at her ass. She had on some lime-green stretches. "Dear lil boy, hear go yo weed." Once she gave Young Money the weed, he started rolling up. As he was getting ready to spark the blunt, he got a text from Mi-Mi. "Who the fuck is that text'n' yo phone shit I don't know."

"Yea, okay, let me find out." Young Money hit the wood a few times and wiped out.

"You think you always pose to get it yo way," she said as she grabbed his dick and put it in her mouth. As she got her rhythm going, Young Money leaned his head back on his headboard and enjoyed the show.

"Damn to that shit feel good." She was making slurping sounds, licking Young Money up and down. TaTa knew she had some dope head. As she began to deep-throat him, she took him to the back of her throat and kept it there for several seconds. As Young Money was fenna come, she swallowed every last drop of him.

"Umm, taste good," she said. As she was taking her clothes off, Young Money was just looking at her figure. TaTa was a bad bitch. She just lacked some of the qualities he was looking for in a female. Once she got back on the bed, she took his shirt off, then his pants and his boxers. Young Money was still semihard, so she grabbed his dick and rubbed it all over her pussy. Once she saw that it was rock-hard, she straddled him with her tight wet pussy. She started off slow. As she was riding him, she was taking her time grinding back and forth. "Ooh, Young Money, this dick so good. I love this dick," she said as she continued to ride him. She picked up her pace and started bouncing up and down on his dick. Ooow, fuck, you fenna make me come. Oh my god, I'm coming, Young Money. Fuck." TaTa kept riding him, catching back-to-back orgasm. As she was climaxing, he let off a fat nut inside her. "Wooh, shit, now that was some bomb-ass sex," she said, all sweaty. Her eddies was sticking to her head. Young Money was still inside her.

Once she got up, she went to the bathroom to go wipe off. Once she wiped off, she brought out a warm face towel to wipe him off. As she was wiping him off, his dick started getting back hard. "Uhahu, don't even start, lil nasty." She went to go put on her clothes. Once she put on her clothes, Young Money threw on some basketball shorts and walked her to the door. "I guess I ain't gonna see you until gods know when."

"You gon' see me shit how you just put it on me. You can see me right now," he said and slapped her on her ass.

"You play too much, but we gon' see if you 'bout what you be talking 'bout."

"Don't even trip. I got you."

As he closed the door behind her, Shota called his phone. "What's the deal?"

"Shit, I'm pullin' up to yo house right now. Meet me in the parking lot."

Young Money threw on a shirt and put his Gucci flip-flop on. When he seen Shota pull up, he got in the car. "What it's looking like?" Young Money said. Shota reached behind and grabbed his Louis backpack and handed it to him. "It's like $250,000 in that bag."

"Get you, my nigga. I'm out a here. I'ma tap in wit you in a few."

"Aight, big cuz, be smooth." Young Money got out the car and went back to the house. Once he got to his room, he dumped the money on his bed. He was just staring at all dem blue strips after he got out of his daze. He counted the money all over again with the money counter he purchased online. The count came out to the same. Once he seen everything was there, he split the money three ways. The split came out to $83,000 apiece. Young Money FaceTimed Jay and Money at the same time. "Wassup wit you, niggas?"

"I'm out here gettn' money." He flipped the cam'ra around and showed them all the stacks of money.

"Oh shit, that's all us right there," Money said.

"Okay, that shit looking real nice," Jay butted in.

"You niggas need to hurry up in come get yall doe. I got shit to do, matter of fact. Money, I'ma just put that shit in yo room in y'all can just do y'all. I'm fenna go fuck wit baby."

"You o cup caken' ass nigga kick rocks."

Young Money hung up the phone on dem niggas. Once he got dressed, he left the house and headed to Mulan's house.

He grabbed a bottle of duce and cracked it open and took a deep swig. "Wooh, dat shit ain't no joke. Let me show you how it's done," Mulan said as she grabbed the bottle out his hand and took two big gulps.

"Okay, turn up, best friend," Fendi said the music playlist she had selected was playing throughout the bus. Mulan was shaking her ass all on Young Money. It seemed like they were the only one on the bus; they were in they on world. Chanele, Fendi, and everybody else were enjoying themselves.

"Fuck it up mu fuck it up," Chanele said as she was on Instagram live. Mulan was all over Young Money. Fendi went to get some drinks from the bar. "Wassup wit you in my sis? Why y'all actn' all anti wit each other?"

"You should ask her that."

"Y'all both on some otha shit, but anyway, wassup wit yo nigga Money."

"Want you go ask him why you acting all scary?"

"Boy, ain't nobody scared. I have dat lil boy pussywiped."

"Ayy, Money, Chanele over here freestyling like she a have you pussy whipped."

"What?" Money got up and walked towards them.

"So what you was sayn you know you can't fuck wit me boy, you can't fuck with me."

"Yea, we gon' see before tonight over." After he said that, he went to go break up the trance Young Money and Mulan were in. "Damn, you lil freaks, save some for the room. Mulan was straddled on top of Young Money tonguing each other down. "Anyway, stupid, we hear the bus fenna pull up to the club right now."

They finally stepped back into reality and headed off the bus. Once they approached the entrance, the bouncer was asking for IDs, and Young Money and Money and shout out, "To my cuz, this bitch finally grown. It's her b-day in we fenna be turned the fuck up. Ain't that right, BF?" She put the cam'ra on Mulan. Once she did that, Mulan started twerkn'. "Ayy, fuck it up, best friend. It's yo b-day."

After they got off Instagram live, they finished getting dressed. "So what club is we going to?" Chanele said.

"I think Young Money got us VIP at the weekend."

"Okay, it's lit. We fenna be actin' up, so what he give you for yo birthday," Fendi said as she was flat-ironing her hair.

"Girl, I don't know. He on some secretive as shit. He talking 'bout the he gone give it to me at the end of the night. So I'm just waiting."

"Yea, because I got to see what he gon' give you because I know dat nigga Jay gon' get me somthen' nice."

"You bitches be suckn' yall niggas." Chanele said.

"Girl, duhh," Fendi said. "If you knew better, you a do better. You betta stop playn' in snatch dat nigga money in he cute. He lucky I got at Jay first, or he would of been all in this pussy."

"Do you gotta be such a slut?" Mulan said.

"Girl, by like I said you need to get at dat nigga."

"Yea, I'ma see wassup."

"Y'all almost ready 'cause I'm supposed to be meeting Young Money in the lobby."

"Yea, we ready. We waiting on you. You the one taking all fucking day," Fendi said.

As they were walkin' out the hotel room, Mulan FaceTimed Young Money. Ring, ring. "Wassup, babe? Where you at?"

"Shut we walking towards the lobby right now."

"Okay, I see you killen' um."

"You see me, babe," Mulan said as she did a 360 with the camera. "Aight, I'ma see you when we get to the lobby."

Once everybody met up, they walked out to the party bus. "Thank you, babe," Mulan said.

"What's that for?"

"Jus' for being you. I really do appreciate you."

"I appreciate you too. Now let's get on this bus in turn up."

He grabbed Mulan by the hand and walked on the bus. It was bottles of duce in ace of spades everywhere. Young Money and Jay weren't twenty-one, so the ID they did have wasn't gon' get them in. "Look, big man, today my girl b-day. We just tryna get in and have some fun. I paid for VIP in all lat, and I gotta few hunned if you let me in my niggas in."

"How much you gon' give me?" the bouncer said.

"Young Money gave him a few hunned."

Once they entered the club, the scenery was lit. It was definitely turned up in that thang. As they got escorted to their VIP area, Young Money stopped and talked to the host about the bottle service. Once he had that taken care of that, he headed to where everybody was at. He instantly rolled up a wood and got it cloudy. Mulan, Chanele, and Fendi were getting it, and they was cuttn' up. As they were dancing, the bottle service was coming wit lit-up bottles of rosey. "Oow, bitch, look at that shit," Fendi said to Mulan.

"I know we lit. I'm fenna go live."

Once she went live, everybody was showing out for the gram. "Yea, you know me in my nigga T'd up. We lit is fuck. Fucking shit up, yea, all lat, and its my b-day. I'm fenna get some dick in my life." Once she said that, Young Money looked at her with a smile on his face. He was waiting for the day; she was ready. Bottles after bottles after bottles were going up. Everybody getting drunk, all the dancing in the world, everybody was on their ass, especially Mulan. She was definitely feelin' it as the club let out and all-white rolls pulled up. Young Money had rented it for the night. The chauffeur got out of the car and opened the back door. As he did that, Young Money grabbed Mulan's hand and escorted her to the car. Mulan couldn't believe it; she had her hand covering her mouth.

"I see you, brother. You came through," Fend said. As they got in the car, the chauffeur asked them where too.

"Just ride around for a minute and drop us off at the spot I told you," Young Money said.

Young Money popped a bottle of Ace of Spades and poured him and Mulan a glass of champagne. "Okay, I see you can be a gentleman when you want to."

"Yea, you know how I do. You know my style. I do anything to make you smile."

"Who you think you is 50 Cent."

"Nah, I'm dat nigga."

As they pulled up to the cosmataligin, Mulan had said, "I thought we was going back to the MGM."

"Just chill. Let me do this. I got it."

Once the driver opened the door for them, Young Money tipped him and grabbed Mulan by the hand and walked inside the hotel. Once they got to the room, Mulan couldn't believe her eyes. There were candles lit everywhere, the lights were dim, and the mood was set just right. "You really tryna make a bitch fall in love. This is so romantic. Thank you, babe," she said, then locked her arms around his waist and started kissing him real passionately.

"Hold on, speed racer." He broke their kiss full back. "You made me want, so I'ma make you want it."

She started to whine. "But I want you right now."

"And I do too, but I got a nice hot bubble bath waiting for us."

As they walked to the master bedroom, there was a big Jacuzzi bathtub in the center of the room. Young Money started taking off his clothes and hopped in. As he hopped in, Mulan followed suit. She slid out her dress, revealing her black bra and black laced thong. She was looking at Young Money all seductive, walking towards him. "Is this what you want?"

"Hell yea, you already know dat I been waiting for this forever."

"Have you?" she said as she began taking off her lingerie and got in. "Ooh, this shit out. What? You tryna boil chicken in this thang." Young Money started laughing.

"Bring you sexy ass over here."

Mulan sat in between his legs, and they were just enjoying each other. As he began rubbing on her titties, Mulan let out a deep sigh. Once he continued doing that, he reached down to her pussy and started rubbing on her clit. "Ooow, babe, that feel so good."

"You like when I rub on yo pussy."

"Uh huh." She shook her head up and down. After they were done wit the foreplay, they got out the tub and dried off. Mulan was low-key nervous. "I can't believe I'm really 'bout to lose my virginity!" As she leaned back on the bed, Young Money asked her if she was ready. She shook her head up and down. "Just don't hurt me, 'kay?"

"I'm not. I promise." He started kissing her real soft and passionately on her lips down to her neck, then ventured off to her titties. He kissed and sucked both titties one by one. He had Mulan going crazy. The pleasure she was receiving was all new to her. Once Young Money went down to her pussy and started licking and sucking on her clit, she couldn't hold back any longer.

"Oh my fucking god, what is you doing to me? Fuck dat shit feel so good." As he kept sucking on her clit, Mulan was getting louder and louder. "Oh my god, I'm fenna cum. I'm cumming. Oh fuck, I'm cumming," as she was having back-to-back orgasm. As she finally caught her breath, Young Money climbed on top of her and slid inside, but because she was so tight, it took him some time. But once he got all the way inside, Mulan took in a deep breath.

"You all right?"

"Yes." As he began his rhythm, Mulan was going crazy. "Ooow my god, babe, it hurt."

"You want me to stop?"

"No, keep going. Please keep going. You feel so good."

Once he sped up, Mulan dug her nails in his back. Young Money let out a small sigh. But he wasn't tripn'. He was lost in ecstasy. "Damn, babe, this pussy so good. You bet not give this pussy to nobody."

"Uh huh, I'm not. Ooow fuck, I'm fenna cum. Young Money, this yo pussy, I promise. Ooow my god, I'm cumming." After several different rounds, they both were tapped out.

"What you thinking 'bout?" Young Money asked Mulan as she was lying on his chest.

"I don't know. I mean, a lot."

"A lot like what?"

"A lot like I just lost my virginity too you, and that should let you know how I fuck wit you, and I just don't want you to hurt me. Like I know you be havn' yo lil bitches calling yo phone, but all that shit fenna be over wit. You are my nigga now, and I don't do no sharing, so I'ma give you some time to send them bitches on they way."

"I got you." After he said that, he got out the bed and went to go grab something out of his pants pocket. When he got back in the bed, he handed Mulan her gift.

"What's this?"

"Open it up and see."

As she opened up the lil gift-wrapped box, tears came to her eyes. It was a 4-karat diamond ring. "Thank you, baby. I love it. Let me find out you ready to get married."

"I mean, not quite yet, but that's a promise ring."

"Oh yeah, so what are you promising me?"

"To always keep it hunnid and to never put no one before you."

"Okay, dat was good, but you forgot one."

"In what's dat."

"To not be fucking wit none of them bumbass bitches cuz I will pull up in beat one of them hoes' ass. Don't let this cute face fool you."

"Man, bring yo crazy ass here." As they embraced, they started kissing and began their sexathon. The next morning, Young Money woke up to Mulan singing in the shower. He looked under the covers and seen light blood spots on the white sheets. He had a big grin on his face. As Mulan came out the shower, she told Young Money to get ready. Their plane would leave in a hour!

Once Young Money got back to the city, he was ready to get back to the money. He was parked in the hood, chillen' to the neck, smoking on some cooks. Ring, ring. "Hello, wassup wit you?" TaTa said.

"Shit cooln' tryna figure some shit out."

"O yea, I'm tryna figure some shit out too, so tell me why I saw you on the gram flexn' wit dat bitch."

"Man, fuck you talkn' 'bout."

"You know what the fuck I'm talkn' bout."

Ayy, Young Money's other line beeped. Mulan was Facetimin' him. He clicked over. "Wassup, babe, what you doing?"

"Nothing, thinking 'bout you on my break. You coming home tonight?"

"You know I'm pullin' up."

"Yea, you betta, and plus I gotta play up for you."

"Is that right?" Now she had his attention.

"Aight, that's wassup. We gon' holla when I get to the spot. All right, baby, talk to you later."

Once he got off the phone, he saw an all-black car riding down the street. His cuzzn Shota was down the street by the basketball court. 'Bout time he could warn him, shots rung off. Bloc, bloc, bloc, bloc. The car sped off. Young Money ran down the street. What he seen was gon' change his life forever. He seen Shota down on the ground, bleeding and coughin' up blood. "No, don't die on me, bra/.I need you." As Shota was coughin', his last words was, "Make shore you get them niggas," then he took his last breath. By the time the ambulance got there, it was too late. Young Money was devastated. He walked to the house with Shota's blood in his shirt. Once he got to the house, he went to his room and grabbed his gloc. He was ready to kill something. Money was blowing his phone up.

As he was fenna get ready to grab his cannon, Wassup, bra?"

"Ayy, my nigga, where you at?" Money said.

"I'm at the house."

"Aight, I'ma fenna pull up on you."

Young Money hung up the phone. His thoughts were everywhere. He was ready to kill something. His big cuzn just got killed, and he couldn't understand what just took place. Money came walking in the house. "Young Money, where you at, bra?" Money had yelled as he walked to the back.

"Ayy, what the fuck, my nigga, you heard what happen?"

"Nigga, fuck heard. I see the whole thing the whip came driving down the street, then all I hear is a gun go off like eight times. I hopped out the car and ran down the street. All I see is this nigga on the ground coughin' up blood." As he was telln' Money, he was tryn' to hold back his tears. "And I'm just looking like what the fuck. All I could tell him was hold on. I heard hella police coming, so I got on."

"Fuck blood dis shit crazy. I can't believe this shit. You know who did this?"

"Nigga, how I'ma know?" They slid straight through out the window and pulled off. "But when I do find out, I'm telln you, my nigga, I'ma smack dat nigga straight up the ambulanes ain't gone be able to save them." Young Money's phone started ringing. "What's good?"

"Shit tryna see wassup wit you," Jay said.

"Man, bra, I'm tryna figure it out. This shit got me fucked up."

"I'm already knowing, so what's the plan?"

"We gon' figure that out when you get here, bet I'm finna pull up."

Young Money hung up the phone. "So look, shit 'bout to get real. My nigga, I ain't doing no playn'. Whoever had so'thing to do wit this shit, I'm telln' you, I'm on dem niggas."

"I'm on the same shit yo on," Young Money said. "First thing first, we gotta get moms up out of here first."

"You know she ain't gon' wonna move."

"I know. We gon' just get her a cool spot out the way, and she still can keep this," Young Money said. Knock, knock. "Go see who that is." Money went to go open the door.

"Wassup, bra, you good?" Jay said as him and Money slapped hands.

"Fuck hah, bra, I ain't. This shit crazy, but shit we gon' figure it out."

Young Money came walking in the living room. "What's the deal, bra? You know I'm on some otha shit right now."

"You in me both."

They sat down on the couch to discuss how they gon' move. "All right, look, we all gotta be on are shit because we fenne move mean on these niggas, so we gotta be smart on how we fenna so about gettn on these suckas," Young Money said.

"I mean to keep it hunned, none of us ain't killed before, but I know all of us already to knock something down, so that's what it is," Money said.

"You nigga know I'm ull in yall, my brothers. We gather money together, in we gon' get on these pussy as niggas together," Jay said.

"Man, this nigg really gone. I can't beleive this shit. I was just wit this nigga," Young Money said.

After they finished discussing how they was gone move, everybody shook hands. "Aight, my nigga, I'm fenna get in traffic," said Young Money. As everybody went their way, he called Mulan. "Wassup, babe."

"Shit chillen' tryna figure some shit out."

"Why you sound like that?"

"Man shit crazy but look though I'm fenna pull up on you."

"Aight, I get off in a minute. I see you when you get home."

After he got off the phone, he went to grab his cannon and got in the car and drove off. Once he got in traffic, he stopped at the store and got some D'usse. After he got some, he drank and drove to the beach. Once he got there, he was sipn' his drank, taking a walk. As he was taking big gulps, he started talking out loud to no one in particular. "How the fuck you gon' leave, bra? What I'ma do now? I guess I gotta finish my breakfast. Don't even trip. I got you, big cuzn." As he took another big gulp from the duce, ring, ring. Mulan was calling him. He ignored the call. As he finished getting his thoughts together, he headed to Mulan's house. Once he got there, he put his house key in the door and walked in the house. Mulan was up watching TV. As he walked to the room, he went to go put his gun up. "Wassup, babe."

"Don't wassup babe me. I was blowing yo phone up all day, so what bitch got you not answer yo phone."

"Man gone with that shit," Young Money said as he leaned back on the bed. "Some shit happened today."

"Speak. I'm listening."

"My cuzn Shota got killed today."

Mulan put her hand over her mouth. "Oh my god, I'm so sorry."

"You don't gotta be sorry. Dem bitch-ass niggas who killed my cuzn gon' be sorry."

Mulan laid her head on his chest. "So what you plan on doing?"

"I'ma body whoever had som'thing to do wit my cuzn getting killed."

"Oh my god, Young Money, please be safe. I really don't want nothing to happen to you. I really care about you. Promise me you gon' be careful."

"Don't even trip, Mu. I'ma be good."

Mulan kissed him on the lips. Once their mouths connected, the passion that they shared between each other was so thick you can cut it with a knife. As they deepened their kiss, Mulan startled Young Money and took off her shirt. Her perky titties were standing at attention. Young Money passionately kissed and sucked both titties. Mulan loved it when he paid attention to her breast. "Umm, dat feel good," Mulan said.

After the light foreplay, it was Mulan's turn to return the favor. As she took off Young Money's shirt, she put kisses all over his chest all the way down to his dick. As she reached it, she put him in her mouth, slowly sucking up and down his shaft. Once she seen he was fully hard, she put his dick inside of her. She winced once her pussy locked on his dick. As she started moving her hips, her pussy was getting wetter and wetter. "Umm, oh my god, babe. You gon' make me come." Mulan moaned. Young Money was lost in his thoughts but still was enjoying Mulan's tight wet pussy. "Oooh shot I love this dick." Once Mulan came, Young Money flipped her over and had her face down, ass up. Once he got back inside her, he started beatn' her pussy up. "Oow fuck, Young Money, huhh I can feel you in my stomach."

"Tell me who pussy this is," he said as he pulled on her hair.

"It's yours. It's all yours," Mulan said.

Young Money was taking all his anger out on her pussy. "Oow, baby, I'm cumming again. Oow why you doing this to me?" Young Money sped up and busted a fat nut inside of Mulan. Once they got done fucking, Mulan laid in his arms.

"Babe, you know I really do care about you," said Young Money.

"Do you really?"

"That's why I need you to make sure you're careful out there, like I know you gotta handle yo business. Just make sure you make it back home to me."

"You know I'ma make it back, but look shit fenna get real, so I need you to be on yo shit out here. You know I don't be having nothing going on, but I hear you," she said after she gave him a kiss on the lips. Young Money got up to go. As he was puttin on his clothes, Mulan asked where he was going.

"I don't know, fenna get in traffic real quick."

"Be careful, okay, and call me once you make it to where you going."

"Aight, I'ma hit you." As he left, he hopped in the whip. Once he got back to the city, he slid through a few hoods and went to the projects. When he got to the hood, he seen Dango coming out the cut. "Wassup, big bra."

"Shit, boy, you know I'm out here. I heard what happen to dat nigga Shota. Dat's fucked up."

"I know, man. Dat shit got me fucked up."

"So what you gon' do about that?" Dango said.

"Man, what you mean? I'm ready to knock one of them niggas down."

"Aight, look, I'ma take you up top up top way where all the suckers was from. We gon' bust our move later tonight like around one a.m. You got you a cannon?"

"Yea, I got one."

"Aight, I'ma hit you in a few," Dango said.

It was almost go time, and Young Money was anxious to get a body. Ring, ring. "Wassup, big bra?"

"Ayy, meet me in back of Da 3."

Once he hung up, he grabbed his gloc 18 and went to go meet up wit Dango. "All right, look, lil bra. We gon' hit the fence at the top of the home. Once we get up there, shoot at anything moving."

Once they made it up top, Dango got in his mode. "Ayy, Young Money, walk on the side of me." As they were creepin' through big block, Dango seen somebody coming out the apartment building. "There you go, lil bra. Get on dat nigga." Young Money didn't hesitate. He let the gloc 18 blow. Flop, flop, flop, flop. He let the whole thirty clips go. "Aight, come on. We gone." Young Money followed Dango back to the hood. Once they reached the projects, they went their separate ways. "Ayy, Young Money, I'm proud of you, lil bra. You did yo shit. Ain't no turning back. You all in now."

"I'm ready. I'm fenna fuck over them niggas." After they went their separate ways, Young Money went to the spot. Once he got in the house, he seen Money on the couch smoking on a wood. "Let me hit that shit."

"Where you was at, bra?" Money said as he passed the wood.

"Man, bruh," he said as he inhaled the cookie smoke. "I just went on a drill wit DDz. I just got all over a nigga up top, put the whole clip on 'em, and you know I had that glock 18 on me."

"Dat was you niggas? Blood, dat's crazy because I heard them shots, and I was thinking to myself, whoever got hit by that shit DOA."

"Yea, man, I got my first body fill me," Young Money said wit a smile on his face.

"Nigga, I'm tryna get me a body too."

"Don't trip, bra. We fenna get on all these niggas."

A week later was the funeral. Everybody showed up. It was like a hood affair. Everybody who had love for him came to pay respect. Young Money and Money had their any camouflage on wit some timbs, the same thing Shota was being buried in. As the service was getting ready to start, the pastor was getting ready to start. "As we gather today to mourn the loss of another black brother because that's who he is, our brother. We all are brothers and sisters, and it's a shame how all this black-on-black crime we have in this community. This is what the devil wants us to do, destroy each other. Amen!"

"Preach, pastor.

"We need to come together and stop this madness. Okay, now do anybody want to say some last close words?" Young Money said his last words. After that, Money said something. Once everybody was done, it was time to view the body. As Shota's mom was getting closer and closer, it seemed like every step she took her legs got weak.

"No, not my baby. Why him, Lord? Take me, please." Young Money seeing his auntie in all that pain made him even madder. He was ready to body sumtn' all over again. Once it was his turn to see Shota in that casket, it brought tears to his eyes.

As he walked towards him, he whispered in his ear, "I got off of dem suckas for you," and walked off once the funeral was over.

They went to the cemetery to bury Shota. Back on the project, Young Money, Money, and Jay were posted in the hood, smoking and drinking. "Look at all these fake-ass niggas, bra. Some these niggas ain't gon' do nothing bout my cuzn being killed. Half these niggas don't even be over here."

"Calm down, nigga. You tripn'. These niggas feel the same way yoo feel," Money said.

"Yea, I hear you, so wassup, you niggas tryna go on a drill tonight? I'm tryna get on some shit."

"You know I'm rockin' wit you. Just let me know when we gon' bust our move," Jay said.

TaTa came walking up. "Wassup, Young Money."

"Shit cooln," he said after taking a gulp of the D'usse.

"Can I talk to you for a min. I gotta take you something that you need to hear."

As they walked off, she started telling him, "I miss you."

"O yea, that's wassup. That's all you got to say. I really been worried about you, all this shit going on around here. I don't want to lose you."

"I thought you had som'thing to tell me."

"Oh my god, I can't fucking stand you. You don't even care about my feelings, but anyway, you know my potna Victoria that stay in Shoreview."

"Yea, what about her?"

"We was turning up and shit, and she started just running her mouth about her nigga Yaya this and that and how he dat nigga and how he got on yo cuzzn."

"O yea, ain't that nigga from Kirkwood."

"Yep, damn, I thought them harbor niggas had som'thing to do with that shit, and I bodied one of them niggas the other day. Oh well, we beefn' wit them niggas anyway he thought to hisself. So let me ask you som'thing, do that nigga be going to her spot?"

"Yea, he be coming over there every now and then."

"Aight, look, I need you to show me where her spot at."

"Aight, but can I get some dick? I been missing you."

"Yep, its good but first, show me where she stay at."

"When you want me to show you."

"Right now."

They hopped in the car and went Shoreview Way right over the hill. Once they slid through, TaTa pointed at the apartment building her friend stayed in. "So this where she stayed," Money said as he slid past her house slowly.

"Yea, it is. Ain't that what I told you."

"Who you talking to?"

TaTa sucked her teeth. "Can I suck yo dick?" Young Money looked at her with a smile on his face.

"Shit, do you?" That was all TaTa needed to hear. She was feelin' for the dick. She grabbed his dick out of his pants and started kissing and licking up and down his dick. As she started deep-throating him, he had to park his car. Once he got back to the projects, TaTa started going crazy. He grabbed the back of her head, fucking her through. As he was fenna cum, she swallowed everything.

"So when I'ma get to see you again?"

"I'ma tap in wit you in a few."

"Yea, I hear. Just be careful out here. I can't lose you foreal."

"Nah, ain't shit like that gon' happen. I know what I'm doing. I got this shit."

TaTa gave Young Money a kiss on the cheek and got out of the car. Ring, ring. Young Money Facetimed Mulan. "Wassup, babe?"

"Nothing fenna get ready to go to work."

"Oh yea, I was just thinking 'bout you seen what you was doing."

"Aww, you was thinking 'bout me wasn't yo cuzzn funeral today."

"Well, yes, man. That shit was crazy. My auntie was crying and shit, but I'm good though."

"Ayy, babe, I gotta play on deck for you. It's something nice."

"Okay, okay, dat's what I'm talking 'bout. We gon' holla. Let me handle my business real quick."

"Aight, babe, be careful and call me when you get in the house."

"Aight, I'ma tap in wit you." As Young Money got off the phone, he got out the car. He pulled up on Money and Jay. "Ayy blood, let me holla at you niggas."

"Where you was at, my nigga?" Jay said.

"Shit bustn' a a few moves checkn' on some shit."

"So what's the word what that bitch TaTa was talking?" Money said.

"Oh yea, man, dat bitch was telln' me how dat bitch Victoria was free-stylen' like that nigga. Ya-ya from the wood was the shooter who killed Shota, and dat bitch TaTa was like dude be over there, and she showed me where the spot was at, so you know we gon' pull up on datt nigga. I'ma do some homework and watch the spot for a few days."

"Okay, dat's wasssup," Jay said.

"So look, once you get the drop, oh o boy, we gon' move on dat nigga."

"Yea, we gon' bust our move, but first, we need to get a stolo," Young Money said.

"My nigga eldarado uncle gotta chop shop. I'ma holla at 'em," Jay said.

"Aight, I'ma tap in wit you niggas in a minute. I'm fenna get in traffic."

Once Young Money pulled off, he sped off in his Panamera. As he was bending laps, he was still trying to understand where everything went wrong. *Damn, we was just getting money together. This shit crazy. It is what it is. I'ma make it shake. I ain't gon' do no playing*, Young Money had thought to himself.

Ring, ring. "Hello, this is Pedro. Ahh, I'm calling on the behalf of Shota. He was a good friend of mine, and we was doing business together. He gave me your number and told me to call you if I couldn't reach him, so can we continue to do business together?"

"Yea, it's good. I'ma let you know when I'm ready for you," Young Money said.

"I think we should meet up. I got something to show you."

"What time you tryna meet up?" Young Money said.

"Meet at nine p.m. at my shop 18th and Mission. Aight, I'ma hit you later."

Money and Jay were still in the hood thuggin'. Everybody was still outside. "Ayy, bra, you know you my nigga," Jay said.

"Yea, I hear you, and I know you swervn' too, but look, I can't wait till Young Money get the drop on dat nigga. I'm ready to body som'thing, man. Who you telling we definitely gotta get on dat nigga."

"Ayy, Money, so once we get on this nigga, we gotta get back to dat bag a nigga money runnen' low. I got like a hunned thou left."

"What you been doing with yo money, man, bra?"

"I been spending hella money, then this bitch Fendi always wanna go shopping. This shit crazy."

"That sound like a personal problem." Money had chuckled.

"But real shit, I was thinking the same thing. We gon' holla at Young Money after we finish handling business." As Money was talking to Jay, a car came flying down the street.

"Ayy, that's them suckas," somebody yelled out. Money had seen the car flying down the street. He knew they was gon' drive up Polau that was in the back of Oakdale, so before the car made it up that way, Money ran to the back and let off his whole clip. Bloc, bloc, bloc, bloc, bloc, bloc. Fuck, he ran back through the cuts. Money ran to his house. Once he got there, he hopped in the shower to wash off the gunpowder. After he finished, he got dressed and drove to Mi-Mi's house.

Young Money was on his way to meet up wit Pedro. *I wonder what the fuck this nigga wonna holla 'bout. I hope he got som'thing good to tell me*, he thought to hisself. Ring, ring. "Ayy, Pedro, I'm outside."

"Good, buddy, I'ma buzz you in."

Once Young Money got buzzed in, Pedro shook hands. "What's going on, my friend? I heard a lot about you. Your cuzn Shota told me a lot about you."

"So wassup? What you wanted to talk to me about?"

"Huh, I see you ready to get down to business."

"Yea, I got shit to do as you can see."

"Okay, let's get straight to business. So look, as you can see, I own my own jewelry store, and I know you be coming up on a lot of jewelry, so if you happen to come across some more, I want to buy all of it."

"It's all good. I'ma tap in when I bust my next move, but as of right now, I ain't on no get money shit. I'ma tryna knock this nigga down that killed my cuzn."

"I think I can help you with that. Follow me."

Young Money followed Pedro to the back of the shop. As he entered, he couldn't believe his eyes. He seen all types of guns from glocs to Drakos, mini mio, and silencers. "Now this what the fuck I'm talking 'bout," he said as he was finger-fucking the Drako. "So how much you gon' charge me for some artillery?"

"Ooh, just take what you need, and we can discuss numbers later."

"Aight, I just need a few handguns and some silencers, and I be good to go."

Pedro grabbed everything he needed. "Hey, Young Money, what's not seen or heard can't be caught. Remember that. Hurry up and handle your business so we can get this money."

"Don't even trip. I'ma do my thing, and everything gon' be Gucci."

It was time to handle business. Young Money finally had got the drop on ol' boy who killed Shota. He had been watching the spot, and he had the coming and going of his victim. "Look, bra, soon as this nigga come out, we gon' blitz this nigga," Young Money said to Money and Jay. They all had glock 23" with silencers and were ready to kill. Once Young Money seen Ya-Ya coming out the house, they all got out the car, and before you knew it, it was guns blazing. Bloc bloc bloc bloc bloc bloc. Once he fell to the ground, Young Money, Jay, and Money stood over him and overkilled him. Once they finished, they walked back to the whip and pulled off.

"Now that's what the fuck I'm talking 'bout. We just bodied that nigga," Jay said.

"Chill out, bra," Young Money said as he was bending corners. "We fenna go dump this whip, and we gon' go to my bitch house in the town." Once they took the car to the chop shop, they left it and got in a rental car. "Y'all know shit fenna get real. We just knocked down one of they shooters, so dem niggas gon' be ready to kill, so we gotta stay on are shit," Money said.

"I keep it on me," Young Money said.

"Ayy, I gotta question, so since we took care of business, can we get back to the bag because a nigga fund's running low," Jay had said. Everybody had to laugh at that.

"Man, you ain't never lied. It's been a heated few weeks, but we handled business, so I'ma holla at Mulan, se wassup wit a play," Young Money said. Once they pulled up, Young Money parked the whip. Once they got out the car, they went in the house. Young Money went to his room to put his new Glock 27 he went to go pick up from Pedro. After the play, they just put down.

"My nigga, I'm hungry is fuck," Money said as he went to go see what was in the refrigerator. He grabbed the Minute Maid kiwi strawberry and poured a cup of juice. Mulan came walking in the house. She seen Money in her kitchen and Jay on her couch.

"I see y'all made y'all self right at home."

"Wassup, sis?" Money said as he put the juice back in the refrigerator. Mulan shook her head and went to her room.

"Hi, babe, I didn't even know you were here. I seen yo greedy-ass brother all in my kitchen," she said as she was taking off her scrubs. She stripped naked and went to go hop in the shower. As she was walking off, Young Money was staring at her figure.

Damn, she sexy is fuck, he thought to himself. He followed her lead and took of his clothes and went to go get in the shower.

As Young Money got in, Mulan jumped. "Oow, babe, you scared me." He wrapped his arms around her as the hot water was running over their bodies.

"It's just me, babe. What you thought? The boogie man was coming to get you?" he said as he started kissing her neck.

"Um, dat feel good, babe. Is that right?" Once he had her going, he started rubbing on her clit. "Oh my god, babe, you fenna make me cum. Oow, shit, I'm cumming." As Mulan came, Young Money washed off and got out the shower.

"Uh ah, where do you think you going? How you gon' get me all started and stop?

"Don't trip, babe. I'ma get you right once you get out the shower." Once Mulan heard that, she finished washing up. She got out the shower soaking wet. Young Money was lying down on the bed with his boxer briefs watching the sports center. As Mulan was drying off, Young Money couldn't keep his eyes off her. Once she finished drying off, he stood up and approached her and started kissing her passionately all the way to the bed. As Mulan leaned back, Young Money was on top of her. His dick was rock-hard, teasing her love box. As he continued to kiss her, he gave her titties some attention. He sucked and licked each breast one by one. As he kissed down her stomach, Mulan let out a slight moan from the pleasure she was receiving from Young Money. Once he reached her clitoris, he licked and kissed it real gentle. As he got his rhythm going, he had Mulan screaming to the high heavens. "Ooow, babe, you gon' make me cum. Yes, right there." Young Money was eating her pussy like it was his last meal. Once Mulan came several times, she was begging him to be inside her. "Babe, I want you inside me."

"You want me inside you?" he said as he was towering over her.

"Yes! you got me so wet." As he slid inside Mulan, holy shit, she gasped for air because of his size. He was huge. "Yes, fuck me. Ooow, you feel so good." He was fucking the shit out of her. Once she came, Young Money busted a fat nut inside her. They both were out of breath. Mulan lay her head on his chest. "Damn, babe, you was doing yo thang," she said.

"I was, huh, I been missing you. It's been mainy these last couple of weeks, and I know we ain't been spending no quality time together."

"It's okay, babe. I know you been handling business, but yea, we been missing you. What you mean we?"

"Um, I been meaning to tell you I'm pregnant. I think it happened in Vegas. The doctor said I'm four weeks. It's just been so much shit going on with you. I didn't know how to tell you. I mean, that's a big surprise."

"So you mean you not mad at me?"

"Why would I be mad at you?"

"I mean, I'm kinda caught off guard, but it's whatever you want to do."

"I want to keep it," Mulan said.

"I see you didn't waste no time figuring it out."

"Nope, I had my mind made up the day I found out, and if you was gon' tell me you wasn't ready, I was still gon' keep my baby."

"Don't trip, babe. I got you. I mean us," Young Money said, smiling, rubbing Mulan's stomach. As she was lying down on Young Money's chest, in her own world, he broke her out her thoughts. "Ayy, babe, let me ask you something." She looked up at him with that "What now?" look. "Why you lookin at me like that?" he said.

"Because you always up to something. Now what's on your mind?"

"You already know I'm tryna get to that bag. I mean, I still got some doe, but I need more. We gotta eat, and plus we gotta lil one on the way."

"You know I got some plays for you. I was wondering when you was gon' say something I thought you was going soft on me."

"Ha, you hella funny. You know I'm trained to go, but what you got on deck though?"

"Okay, so look, one of my aunties and her husband own a jewelry store in Chinatown."

"Oh yea, that's gon' be a lay up me and my niggas running in that bitch."

"It's not gon' be that easy. It's a security guard that be at the front of the door, so you gon' have to figure it out."

"I got it, babe. I'm fenna go holla at these niggas real quick." Young Money got up and went to the living room. Money and Jay were watching sports center, smoking on some gilado. "Let me hit that shit," Young Money said as he inhaled the smoke and exhaled. "Y'all niggas ready to get paid?"

"My nigga, you know we ready to get to it," Jay said.

"What the lick read?" Money said.

"It's a jewelry store in Chinatown. I'ma do my homework on it, and I'ma let y'all know wassup. Aight, that's wassup. I'm fenna get up out of her. That bitch Fendi fenna come get me. Let me find out you fillen' baby," Young Money said.

"And wassup wit you in Channele."

"I mean, we be talking and shit. I ain't really been trippin' off baby like that."

"What? You playing! If I was you, I would of been bent that shit over," Jay said. Knock, knock, knock.

"Bra, who is that knockin' like they the police?"

Young Money went to go look through the peephole. When he seen who it was, he opened the door. "Damn, what took y'all so long to open the door?" Fendi said as she came walking in the house. "And what y'all doing in my cuzzn house? This is not Oakdale."

"Ain't nobody worried about what you talking 'bout," Money said.

"Boy, I know you ain't talking, and wassup wit you in my sister?"

Mulan came walking in the living room. Bitch, I knew I heard yo ass. What you doing over here?"

"Girl, coming to get this nigga," she said, pointing at Jay.

"Okay, I see y'all. Girl, let me talk to you real quick." They walked back to Mulan room. "So wassup?"

"I'm pregnant, girl."

"By who?"

"Bitch, don't play with me. You know the only nigga hittn' this is Young Money."

"So is you keepn it because that nigga getting money."

"Yea, I'm keepin it, and it ain't about his money. I get my own money."

"Well, okay, Ms. I Get My Own Money. Shit, I get my own money too, but a lil extra ain't gon' hurt."

"Girl, bye, you something else," Mulan said, chuckling. "And what you got going on anyway?"

"Girl, I was coming over here to pick my babe up, and plus you just gave me some tea, and I'm happy for you, cuz." She gave Mulan a hug. "Aight, girl, I'm fenna get up out of here. Me and Jay fenna go work on our baby."

"You is so nasty."

"Bitch, you ain't fenna be the only one getting pregnant by a nigga that's getting money."

"But it's not even 'bout his money. I really love him," Mulan said.

"Well, I love money, cash money, and Jay got that, so I'm fenna lock him in."

"Aight, girl, call me when you get home. I mean, after you finish making yo baby."

"Bitch, bye! I'ma call you."

Fendi left out. "This bitch is crazy. She know damn well me and mines rockn' that nigga know wassup," Mulan was thinking out loud.

"Wassup, babe," Young Money said as he walked in.

"Nothing, talking to Fendi crazy ass."

"Oh yea, what yall was talking bout?"

"I was just telling her that I was pregnant. She was happy for me."

"Come here." Young Money wrapped his arms around her waist. "You know I love you."

"I love you too, babe.

"I want you to know I got us. I'ma do everything in my power to take care of us," said Young Money.

"Just make sure you make it home to me. Don't let none of them niggas steal you. I don't know what I would do without you."

"Don't trip, babe. I got this shit. I know what I'm doing."

"But look, I need you to show me where that spot at you was telling me about."

"Okay we can do it on my lunch break, so just come pick me up."

"Aight, I'ma tap in wit you in a minute. I'm fenna go drop my brother off in the city. I hit you when I get out there." Young Money gave her a kiss and left out.

* * *

The next day came around, and Young Money was ready to do his homework; he went to go pick up Mulan from work. "Hi, babe," Mulan said, then gave him a kiss. "How yo day going at work?"

"It's going good. I can't wait to finish these classes so I can get my RN certificate and be working in a hospital."

"It's gon' happen. You just got to be patient."

"Turn right here," Mulan said.

Young Money parked. He put his fitted hat on and a chain he had got from his cuzzn Shota. "I be right back." As he walked in, the security guard was on high alert.

The guy that was over the counter greeted him in broken English, "Hi, can I help you."

"Yea, you can. I was looking for something nice for my girlfriend."

The Asian dude knew Young Money had some type of money from the chain he was wearing. "Oh, you have girlfriend. I have nice things for girlfriend. Come see."

"And you can clean this for me. It need a lil touch-up."

"Okay, I clean for you, and you look for you girlfriend." Young Money seen a 24K gold carat locket, and that was what he was gon' get Mulan. The Asian guy came from the back cleaning the chain.

"Did you like anything?"

"Yea, I'm feelin' that gold locket."

"Oh, you like the locket. It's 1,100 hundred dollars. You have money?" Young Money pulled out a loaf of money. From the sight of the money, the Asian eyes grew big. He pulled off eleven blue strips. "You sure that's all you want?"

"Yea, I'm good. Can you put that in a gift box?"

Once the Asian put the chain in the gift box, he gave Young Money back his chain. As he was leaving, the Asian said, "When you come back, I'ma have more for you to look at."

"I be back real soon," he said under his breath.

Once he got back in the car, Mulan asked him, "So what you think?"

"Man, babe, that shit gon' be a layup. We in that bitch next week."

"So you gone be able to get in and out?"

"That's how I'm doing it."

"Good, make sure you take everything."

"You know I'm fenna be like the grinch in that bitch."

"Yo ass crazy," Mulan said as she was laughing. As Young Money dropped Mulan back off at work, he was getting ready to slide to the projects. "Is you coming home tonight?"

"I might. I gotta handle some business, but if I don't, I'll let you know."

"Aight, call me." Mulan gave him a kiss and went back to work.

Young Money FaceTimed Money. "Wassup, scrub, where you at?"

"Shit in the hood."

"Where in the hood?"

"I'm in the house."

"Aight, I'm fenna pull up on you." Once Young Money got to Oakdale, he drove to the house that was an off street inside Oakdale projects.

When he pulled up, he seen Money standing outside of his car talking to the thugs. "Wassup wit you, niggas," Young Money said.

Money had walked over to the car. "Wassup, bra? What's the word?"

"Get in real quick." As Money got in, Young Money drove off. "You got some dro, my nigga?" Young Money asked Money.

"Yepp, but we need to stop at the store real quick," he said. They stopped at the Q Street Store. As they were pulling up, they seen them suckas driven' down Third Street. "A blood you seen them suckas just drive past," Money said. "You got yo cannon on you?"

"You know I keep dat thang on me." Young Money pulled out the FN out the tuck spot.

"Oow, okay, I see you."

As Money went to go get the wood, Young Money FaceTimed Jay. "Wassup, nigga? Where the fuck you been at?"

"Nigga, where you been at? I'm at where I'm at, and I'ma be where I be."

"My nigga, if you don't get the fuck out of here, niggas already know where you been at."

Money had got back in the car. "Who is that?"

"That's this nigga Jay."

"All pussy niggas be having they phone on silent and shit. Let me find out Fendi got that ass on lock," Money said. "Wassup wit you weird-ass niggas anyway over their looking like the doublement twins?"

"My nigga, we tryna bust this play. We fenna pull up on you," Young Money said.

"Shit, say no more. Pull up then."

Once they hung up, they slid to the town. When they got to Jay's spot, Young Money called his phone. "Come outside, bra."

"Aight."

Once Jay got in the car, he started talking 'bout the play. "So wassup? What?"

"The lick ready. Come on, man. You know I got sumthin' on deck," Young Money said as he inhaled the cookie smoke. But check it out." Once he said that, he had their attention. "It's a jewelry store."

"Bra, we ain't never hit no jewelry store," Money said.

"Well, nigga, we do now, but like I was saying, it's a jewelry store inside Chinatown. It's one security guard, but he don't carry no gun, so look, this how we gon' do it. It's a alleyway. We gon' park the car there the jewelry store on the corner. We gon' blitz that bitch. Jay, you gon' take care of the security guard and make sure nobody comes in." Jay nodded his head. "Money, you gon' take care of the Asian nigga at the counter, make sure he don't try no funny shit. And me, I'ma smash all the jewelry cases and get all the gold. While I'm doing that, Money, take the China boy to the back and make him open up the safe. We in and out, so that's the play. We gon' bust our move Monday morning at eight a.m."

"Okay, that's wassup. How much you think is in there?" Jay said.

"Shit, yo guess is good as mine. We gon' find out." They all started laughing. "So everybody know they position. We in and out. This gon' put us over the hump."

"Yea, nigga, how many times you gon' tell us?" Jay said.

"But check it out. That bitch Mi-Mi and Stacy throwing a party at Airbnb in Concord is we pullin up."

"Nigga, you know we pulln' up. What time that shit start?" Young Money said.

"Like around ten p.m."

"Aight, we gon' meet up in the projects."

"Ayy, Jay, you sure Fendi gon' let go out the house tonight?" Money said.

"Fuck you mean, she can't tell me nothing."

"Yea, aight, nigga, say that." Then everybody shook hands and went their way.

Later that night, everybody was dressed to impress. Young Money had on a Gucci T-shirt with the Gucci jacket and pants to match. Jay had on all Balmain head to toe, and Money had on a Louis Vuitton collar shirt, Louis glasses, all-black robin jeans, and some red bottom sneakers. As they pulled up to the party, it was live, and music was blasting! Bitches were walking in. "Y'all ready to go be some starz in this thing?" Young Money said. They all got out the whip with they G-mans tucked in they waist. G-mans is a slang for Glock handguns. As they approached the party, the young hoes were thirsty to get they attention.

"Oow, bitch, that's them Oakdale niggas. I heard them niggas getting money," one girl said as she was waiting in line to get in the party.

"That ain't the only thing I heard they be doing."

"Bitch, what you heard? Tell me," the girl standing in line said.

She wispered in her ear, "Girl, I heard them niggas be killing people. Bitch, swear da god."

"Well, I don't care about none of that shit. I'm tryna fuck wit one of them niggas."

Once Young Money and them walked in the party, all eyes were on them, courtesy of the bust-down jewelry they had on. "Ayy, it's lit in this thang," Jay said.

"It's definitely lit in this thang, bra. I'm fenna turn up fashowly," Money said.

"Yea, I hear you, niggas, but I'm tryna get faded pop open that D'usse."

"Oh, thirsty-ass nigga," Jay said as he opened the d'usse, and they was peepn' the scenery. They had the D'usse in rotation.

Mi-Mi was feeln' herself. She was off a uro one of the purest ecstasy pills. "Best friend, our party lit. I know I didn't know all these people was gone show up," Stacy said.

As they was viben' to the music, Mi-Mi spotted Young Money on the other side. "Bitch, look who in here."

Stacy was sipn' on her drink. "Bitch, who is you talking bout?"

"You don't see Money and Young Money over there with that other light-skinded boy, and who the fuck is them bitches all over our niggas?"

"I don't know, but let's go start some shit," Stacy said.

As they approached them, Mi-Mi cleared her throat. "Wassup wit y'all. Young Money, you not gon' tell me happy birthday?"

"Oh shit, today yo birthday? Happy b-day, lil baby."

"I mean, you would of knew if somebody picked up the phone."

"I ain't gon' lie, I been busy is fuck these past few weeks."

"Yea, I hear you," Mi-Mi said. The other girls that was talking to Young Money and them was getting annoyed. Mi-Mi seen one of the girls roll her eyes. "Bitch, what is you rolling yo eyes for because if it's a problem, we can get it poppn'. Matter of fact, you bitches can get the fuck out my party." She went to go get the security. "Wassup, Money," Stacy said.

"Shit cooln'. Wassup wit you. How you been?"

"Just working and missing you. Why haven't I heard from you?"

"I been having hella shit going on."

"I heard what happened to yo cuzzn."

"Yea, everything cool though. We took care of it."

"Please be careful out here. I don't want nothing to happen to you."

"I'ma be good. Don't trip, but you looking cute. I see you check you out."

He had Stacy blushing. "So is you staying after the party? We having a sleepover when everybody leaves."

"O yea, you know I'm in here. I ain't going nowhere." As Mi-Mi came back with the security, she was talking hella shit.

"So what you was saying the girl was quite?" One of the girls that knew Mi-Mi was tryna plead her case. "Mi-Mi, why is you doing all that?"

"Because I don't like that bitch attitude, and she lucky I'm looking all cute right now, or I would of beat her ass and put her out myself. So with that, y'all can leave with this bitch, or y'all can stay, but she gotta go."

The girl looked at her so-called friends. "So y'all not coming with me?" They just looked at her.

"Okay, time's up. You gotta go." Security escorted the girl out the party. Her so-called friends walked off.

"So back to you. Young Money, you better stop playing with me."

"Man gon' wit that shit, you siked out."

"Oow, that's my song." She grabed Young Money to the dance floor and started twerking on him. As he was dancing, Jay grabbed a girl who was just looking around. Not the one to be outdone, he had to turn up with his nigga. Money and Stacy followed suit; they all were enjoying the moment. Everybody was drunk and high as the party was winding down. People were leaving, and the ones who were staying were arguing over the rooms.

"I know one thing. Me and my nigga is going to my room," Mi-Mi said as she grabbed Young Money, then walked to the room. As she entered, she instantly dropped to her knees and unbuckled his Gucci belt and put his dick right in her mouth. As she was licking the shaft up and down, she put him all the way to the back of her throat, and she begun to gag. That turned her all the way on, so she continued what she was doing.

In the other room, Money and Stacy were passionately kissing. "Um, Money, I love you so much. I want you to make love to me," Stacy said in between kisses. As Money continued kissing, he started putting kisses on her neck. He started taking piece by piece of clothing off. Once Stacy was completely naked, he admired her body.

Jay was downstairs on the couch getting it in wit some big booty bitch that he had face down ass up. "Ooow, shit, right there. I'm fenna cum." As Jay continued beating her pussy up, him and the girl both came at the same time.

Young Money was driving Mi-Mi crazy. He was beating her lil tight pussy up missionary style. "Damn, girl, this pussy good."

"Oow, Young Money, it's all yours. This yo pussy. You can have it when you want."

When he heard that, he flipped her over, and she assumed the position facedown ass up. As she was throwing it back, Young Money was slapping her ass and pulling on her hair. Mi-Mi was enjoying every minute. "I'm fenna cum. Oh fuck, I'm cuming." Mi-Mi's pussy was soaking wet. As she was cumming back-to-back, Young Money sped up his pace and busted a fat nut inside her. Once he was done, he fell out. Money was making sweet passionate love to Stacy. Both their heartbeats were in sync. She had her arms wrapped around his neck, and her legs were wrapped around his waist. "Money, I love you so much."

"I love you too, babe. Fuck, this pussy so good."

"You love this pussy."

"Yea, I do."

"Well, give me a baby." As Money continued making love to Stacy, he had her legs shaking. "Oow, babe, I'm cumming." As she was cumming, Money let off a big load deep inside her. As they were done, they lay in each other's arms. Once morning came, Young Money woke up first. "Ayy, wake up," as he nudge Mi-Mi.

"What the fuck? Why is you waking me up this early?"

"Because we fenna go to cuz to get you one of them plan B pills, so go get dress."

"Boy, don't nobody wanna have no baby by you anyway," she said as she put back on her dress.

Once they left, Money and Stacy were just waking up. "Good morning, babe," she said and gave him a kiss on the lips.

"Uh huh, you ain't even brush yo teeth yet."

"Boy, my breath don't stink, and you love this stank breath anyway."

"That ain't the only thing I love."

"Boy, you is so crazy. Who is making all that noise?"

"Ayy, y'all seen Mi-Mi crazy ass last night was wilding out."

"No, I don't give a fuck. That bitch had me fucked up. I don't know who she thought she was, but I ain't the one," she said as she hit the wood and passed it to Jay.

"Why the fuck do you gotta be all loud?"

"Im Mi-Mi, bitch."

"O well, I don't care," she said, moving her neck back and forth. Stacy walked in the kitchen, looking in the refrigerator, grabbing the eggs, hash browns, bacon, and biscuits. Once she grabbed the skillets out the cabinets, she preheated the oven and turned on the stove.

As the food began to simmer in the air, Young Money came walking to the kitchen. "Wassup, sis? I see you throwing down. I know I get a plate."

"I see what I can do."

"My nigga, stop playen'."

"Nah, I got you, brother."

"Ayy, I see dat nigga Money was doing his thang last night."

"Nah, you funny. You betta ask him who the one did they thang."

As Young Money walked off, Stacy continued cooking. "You had fun last night." He had gotten a text from Mulan as he was walking up the stairs to go holla at Money.

"Yep, it was cool."

"So when you coming home?"

"I'm fenna be on my way in a minute."

"Aight, I see you when you get here."

"Yepp, yepp, ayy, babe, can you make me something to eat."

"What you want me to make you?"

"I don't know. Surprise me."

"Aight, I see you later, love you, kisses face emoji."

"Love you more, kissy face emoji."

"Da fuck you in here doing playing with yoself."

"Fuck up out of here siked out as nigga."

"Ayy blood you got Stacy down there cooking breakfast and shit. All you know how I do I did my thing."

"I see. Let me ask you something. You really feeling her?"

"Who?"

"Stacy, dumbass?"

"Oh yea, that's baby. She knows wassup."

"But check it, you ready for tomorrow."

"Hell yea, I'm ready okay. I'm fenna text this nigga Jay to come up here."

Once Jay came in the room, they went over the play. "So look, we gon' bust are move at 8:30 in the morning, but we gone pull up at 7:30 in watch the flow for a minute, so when we go in there, Jay, hold the security guard down. Money, you get on the China boy. Take him to the back and make him open up the safe, and I'ma clear out all the jewelry. So we gon' be good. Let's go get paid." As they shook hands, Stacy was bringing Money his plate.

"All, sis, where my plate at?"

"I put yours in the microwave."

Jay ran down the stairs to go get his plate. As they finished eating, Young Money was ready to go. "Wassup blood we up outta here." He nudged Jay. "Come on. I'm ready to cut. Anyway, go ask that nigga Money if he coming."

"Nigga, you go ask him."

"Bra, why you can't just go ask him?" Young Money said matter-of-fact.

"I know what I'm fenna do." As he was FaceTiming Money, he was talking shit to Jay. "That's why you walking home. Ayy, Money, you coming? Bra, we feena cut."

"No, he not going nowhere. I'ma drop him off," Stacy said."

"Shit, you ain't gotta tell me twice, bra. Tap in."

Young Money hung up the phone and walked towards the door. "Damn, a bitch can't get no hug goodbye."

"Oh, my bad," as he gave her hug and squeezed her ass.

"So I ain't fenna see you for a couple of weeks?"

"Why you say that?"

"You know how you be."

"Man gone wit that shit I'ma pullup on you. Yea, we gon' see."

Once Young Money and Jay left, he got in the car and pulled off. "Ayy, bra, roll some tree up." When Jay finished rolling the wood up, he sparked it up and hit it a few times and started coughing.

"What's this shit? That some dope."

"That's that gilado," Young Money said. As they pulled up to the projects, Jay went to his house, and Young Money went to his. Once he got in the house, his mom was watching the 49ers on TV go touchdown. "Wassup, Ma, what you doing?"

"Boy, watching this football game, and where is yo brother at?"

"He wit his girlfriend," he said as he sat down on the couch.

"And who is his girlfriend? Y'all lil muthafuckas betta be wearing condoms because I ain't got time to be somebody grandma. Boy, why is you looking at me like that?"

"Because I got something to tell you."

"You bet not tell me you got somebody pregnant."

"Yea." Once she heard that, she smacked him in the back of his head. "Just tell me this is it one of these fast lil girls from over here."

"Nah, it ain't."

"Thank God. So who is she?"

"Her name Mulan. She black and Asian."

"You done got a lil mix girl pregnant?"

"Yea, I did, but she different, and I think I love her."

"Boy, you still a baby. You don't know what love is, so what's her mom name."

"Her my name is Yoyo, and she passed when Mulan was sixteen."

"Oh, I'm sorry to hear that. So when I'ma get to meet her?"

"Whenever you want to."

"All right, bring her by next Sunday. We can watch the game, and I'ma cook."

"Ma, I gotta tell you one more thing."

"What it is now, boy?"

"She a Raiders fan."

"Oh, hell nah. She definitely can't come now. But yea, bring her by next Sunday."

Once Young Money was done talking to his mom, he went to his room and took off his clothes and hopped in the shower. As he let the hot water run over his face, he was thinking about tomorrow, and a wide grin came across his face. As he was getting out the shower, his phone was ringing. He seen it was TaTa FaceTiming him. Once she answered, she instantly started talkin' shit. "So bitch you was at them hoe's party last night, and I seen that bitch Mi-Mi all over you oh thirsty ass."

"My nigga, shut the fuck up, and bitch, watch yo mouth. Let another bitch word come out yo mouth, I'ma slap the fuck out of you. I'm saying you know I don't fuck with them bitches. That ain't got shit to do with me but wassup though I got shit to do."

"I need to talk to you about something. It's important, aight. Imma pull up on you tomorrow."

"Why I can't just come to yo house? I know you at home."

"I just told you I got shit to do."

"Oow, I fucking hate you!"

"Yea, I know. I hate me too sometimes." After he said that, he hung up and blocked her from calling for the day. After throwing on his Billionaire Boys Club sweatsuit and spraying on his Gucci cologne, he was done getting dressed. He grabbed his XD glock 23 and headed out the door.

"Son, where you going?"

"To my girlfriend house."

"Okay, be careful."

"Okay."

As he was turning to walk out the door, she stopped him again. "Son, Moma need some money." He chuckled and pulled out a wad of money and pulled off some blue strips. "Thank you, son."

Young Money finally got to his car. He rolled up a wood and pulled off on his way to Mulan's house. As he hit a few lefts and rights, he was going across the bay bridge, checking his rearview mirror, making sure nobody was following him. Once he got to Mulan's house, he parked his car got out and walked up the stairs. As he stuck his key in the door and opened it, he smelled the aroma of good food. "Hi, babe. The food is almost done," Mulan said. Young Money went to the back room to go put his cannon up. When he walked back in the kitchen, he wrapped his arms around Mulan's stomach as she was over the stove putting her finishing touches on the food.

"How is my lil man doing?"

"We doing fine, and how you know its not gone be a girl?"

"Because I just got this feeling you gon' have a boy."

"Well, we gon' see. I think I might have a gender reveal."

"What's a gender reveal?"

"It's when you get some family members together, and you see if it's going to be a girl or a boy."

"Oh, that sound cool. We should do that, and I told my mom about you. She know we fenna have a baby."

"Foreal you told her? What she say?"

"She was trippin at first, but I told her you was the one."

"Yea, okay, I'm the one."

"You know you is, and what you cooking?"

"I cooked some pot roast marinated with some red potatoes, some cabbage, homemade macaroni and cheese, and some corn bread."

"Okay, babe, do yo thang then."

"You see me, you know I be doing my thing when I want to." Young Money slapped her on the ass and went to go watch the game in the living room. As halftime came around, Mulan was setting the table. "Babe, the food ready." Young Money went to the table, but before he was fenna eat, he took a pic of his plate and put it on the gram: "#babe just did her thang she tryna get me fat."

As Young Money took a spoonful, Mulan interrupted. "Uhuhh, boy, you betta bless that good meal I just cooked for you."

"Whatever you say, Mom."

He was eating that food like it was his last meal smacking and everything else you do when you hungry. "I see you was hungry," Mulan said.

"I ain't gon' lie, babe. This shit hella good."

"Thank you, babe. I try."

Once they was finished, Mulan cleared the table and went to go wash the dishes. Young Money was lying down when Mulan came in the room. Just like a black person get full and goes to sleep. "But I'm not done with you yet, so you bet not go to sleep."

"Ain't nobody fenna go to sleep."

"Yea, okay," Mulan said and stripped naked and got in the shower. As she let the hot water run over her body, she squirted some shea butter body wash on her body, scrubbing and rubbing it over her body. Once she got to her stomach, she started rubbing it. She seen that it was getting hard. She dropped a tear because she was happy and sad at the same time. Happy because she was bringing a beautiful child in this world and sad because she couldn't share this moment with her parents. Once she rinsed off, she got out the shower, dried off, and walked in the room. She smacked her lips.

What she saw made her errotated in a smile. She knew she threw down on that meal. Young Money was knocked out snoring, so she gave him a kiss on his lips. When he felt her get in the bed, he wrapped his arms around her stomach and fell back to sleep.

Once the morning came, Young Money was up at 6:00 in the morning, ready to get to it. He washed his face, brushed his teeth, put on an all-black Nike sweatsuit, kissed Mulan, and walked out the door. When he got in the car, he made sure he had one in the head of his XD glock 23 and drove off on his way to the city. As he was crossing the bridge, he called Money. "Wassup, my nigga, wake yo game up. The early bird get the worm first."

"Bra, it's six in da morning. You on some tweaker shit."

"Nah, nigga, I'm on some get money shit, so get ready. I'm getting off the bridge. Call dat nigga Jay and tell him to get ready."

Young Money hung up. As he was getting off the freeway, he hit a few lefts and rights, and he was in the hood. Jay and Money were sitting on the three-story stairs. "Look at this nigga," Jay said as he hit the wood and passed it to Money.

Ring, ring. "What's popn'? Where you niggas at?"

"We right here on the stairs," Money said.

"Wassup, you niggas ready?" Young Money said.

"Nigga, we stay ready. TTY trained to go," they all said at the same time.

"Let me hit that shit." Money hit the wood one more time and passed it. Young Money inhaled the cookie smoke. Once he exhaled, he begun going over the plane once again.

"All right, look, the store open up at eight, so once we get over there, we gon' watch the spot for a minute, and as soon as we see the security guard and the China boy go in, we gon' blitz in right behind them. Jay, you get on the security guard, lay him down, and take his gun off his hip. I got some zip ties for you, so you can tie his arms together. Money, you go after the China, boy grab him, and take him to the back. Make him clear out the whole safe. And I'ma clear out all the jewelry drawers. We in and out two minutes, we gone leave out the back. Let's go get this fucking money."

They all got in a rental car they got with a stolen credit card. Once they reached their destination, it was going on 7:30. They had thirty minutes until go time. "All right, come on, y'all." They all got out of the car, standing on the side of the building with their hoodies pulled tight as they seen the China boy go in first and then the security guard went in last.

Jay went first. As he rushed in first, he took over the situation. "Get the fuck on the ground." Bam! He hit the security guard across the head, knocking him to the ground. Money had the China boy by his shirt with the gun to his head. "Take me to the safe."

"There no safe."

"Whack, bitch, stop playing with me, and show me where the safe at."

"Okay, okay don't kill me."

As Money was in the back, taking care of the business, Young Money was clearing out the jewelry drawers. Money came from the back. "I got everything."

"Come on. We out of here," Young Money said.

They all walked out the back door, got in the car, took their hoodies off, and drove off. They headed to the freeway to go across the bridge. They took a pit stop to switch cars. Once they switched cars, they went to Mulan's house. When they got to Mulan's house, everybody got out of the car and walked in the house. "Ayy, bra, it's som'thing to drink in this bitch," Jay said.

"Nigga, I don't know. Go check," Young Money said as he turned the channel 5 news on.

"Breaking news, it was a robbery in Chinatown at Asian gold jewelry store. They say the suspect got away with a large amount of money in 1.5 million in jewelry. There wasn't no witness, so no one could give no description of the suspects. Back to you, John."

"So word on the street we got 1.5 million in jewelry. I wonder how much Pedro gon' give us for all this, Young Money, and shit, you heard what the news lady said? That shit worth 1.5, so we want at least 1.2," Money said.

"So wassup, you niggas ready to count the bag."

"O yea, I forgot all about that shit," Young Money said. "This nigga siked out, bra."

Jay dumped all the money out on the coffee table, and they all dug in, grabbing stacks of money. After they finished counting the money, the total came out to 450,000. "How much y'all count came out to?" Young Money asked.

"$150,000," Jay and Money said.

"Okay, that's a $150,000 apiece," Young Money said. They all slapped hands.

"We did that shit. Ayy, Money, you seen this nigga Jay? He was all over, dude."

"Man, bra, I had to hit the China boy all in his face. He was acting like he wasn't gon' show me where the safe was at. You siked out, my nigga," Jay said.

"But look, I'm fenna call Pedro to come look at this shit." Young Money FaceTimed him. Ring, ring. "Wassup, buddy, I got something for you to look at."

"O yea, let me see what you got for me." As Young Money was showing him the merchandise, Pedro was getting excited.

"Buddy, don't go nowhere. I'm come to you right now. Where are you?"

"I'm at my girl house."

"Okay, send me the address."

"Aight, I'm fenna do it right now."

Once Young Money got off the phone with Pedro, he texted the number. "Ayy, Jay, call that weed delivery place. A nigga tryna get high. Jay, put the order in."

"You ordered some woods," Money said.

Ring, ring. "Wassup, hey, buddy, I'm outside."

"Aight, come up." Pedro came in the house.

"Wassup, everybody, so where is the good stuff at?"

"Come to the back."

Pedro had a duffle bag full of money. He was ready to spend every dollar. He pulled out the digital scale and weighed the gold. It came out to 10,500 grams. "Wooh, this a lot of gold, my friend. I give you 800,000 thousands."

Young Money smiled. "Nice try, Pedro. See, I watch the news, and they said the gold is worth 1.5 million. I want 1.1 million, and we got a deal."

"Okay, I have 800,000 right now, and I'll give you the rest tomorrow."

"Sounds like a plan to me."

As Pedro was getting ready to leave, Young Money stopped him. "Ayy, Pedro, I need some new toys."

"It's all good. Just stop by the shop."

Once Pedro left, Young Money walked to the living room with a duffle bag full of money and dumped it on the coffee table. "We got more money to count. This 800,000 right here. He owe us 300,000 more, so we eatn'. I'm fenna go get bust down everything. It's time to shit on these niggas."

It was Money and Young Money's b-day, and they were sitting on top of the world literally. They had a president suite at the Trump Tower overlooking Times Square. They had they pre turnup going inside the suite. "Yea, man, this rich nigga shit, you niggas. Don't grind like us, so y'all definitely ain't gon' shine like us. You see us bust down the whole gang here. We in this Trump Tower." Young Money was talking his shit on Instagram live. "Ayy, Money, talk yo shit. Ayy, you see me fifty, for the chain eighty, for the bust-down rolly."

"Hold on, hold on, you niggas ain't the only niggas getting money," Jay said as he pulled out a wad of blue strips and showing off his jewelry.

"Y'all think y'all all that," Fendi said.

"Nah, we know we all that. Ayy, babe, come here. Money, take this picture of us." As Young Money wrapped his arm around Mulan's waist, Money took the picture.

"What time is we leaving?" Chanele said.

"I'm ready to turn up." She was iritated because she liked Money, but she knew Money had a bitch, and to make matters worse, he invited Stacy, and Chanele wasn't feeln' it.

"So how long you in Money been together, girl?" Mulan asked Stacy.

"We been on and off since we was in highs chool. What about you and Young Money?"

"For about six months, and I know what you thinking. How am I pregnant so fast? Why I'm keeping it. So to answer your question, I love him, and everything just feel right."

"That's crazy. I love Money too, and I'm just waiting for my turn to get pregnant.

"Girl, you so crazy right."

"Y'all ready to cut the party bus outside?" Young Money sent everybody and grabbed their coats.

"Damn, its cold is fuck out here," Money said as they got on the party bus. The scenery was looking nice. It was gold bottles everywere. Young Money, Money, and Jay were vibing to the music. They all had gold bottles in they hand, couldn't nobody tell them nothing. They was all getting money. Chanele was feeling herself. She had way too much to drink. She got up and started twerkn'. All eyes were on her.

"Fuck it up, sister," Fendi yelled out she was putting on a show for Money. She knew Money was looking at her, so as she was twerkn', she seductively ficked her lips at him. Once the song was over, she went to go sit down.

"Bitch, you did that on perpose," Mulan whispered to Chanele.

"That nigga know wassup. That bitch ain't fucking with me, period." Mulan couldn't do nothing but laugh. As they pulled up to Club ——, the scene was lit. It was bad bitches and niggas that looked like they were getting Money, and since Young Money, Money, and Jay were still too young to get in the club, that didn't mean they weren't gon' get in. As they by passed the long-ass line and the long faces, Young Money slid the bouncer a band, and they got right in. They all were dressed to impress the host and led them to their seats.

"Can I get y'all some drinks?"

"Nah, lil baby, but you can get us some bottles of some duce in. I want nineteen bottles of some Ace of Spades," Young Money said.

"Okay, but you do know are ace of spade bottles is 2,000 a bottle?"

"Did I ask you the price? I keep that bag on me and then pulled out a wad of money." The hostess was all smiles as she walked off because she knew the commission she was gon' get.

"Bra, did that bitch just try to get at us like we ain't getting money?" Money said.

"Shit, if they didn't know, they 'bout to know now," said Jay.

As the bottles was being brought by some beautiful ladies, the bottles had sparkles like it was the Fourth of July. And too top it off, the DJ gave Young Money and Money a birthday shoutout. Everybody was enjoying themselves. Everybody had a good bottle in they hands except Mulan because she was pregnet. Young Money was smoking on some cooks when some nigga walked over to his section. "Ayy, no disrespect, fam. I'm diggen' you niggas style where yall from. We from Cali. my nigga."

"Okay, that's what I smell in the air. That shit smell good. You got some more of that shit?"

"Yea, I do. Why? Wassup?"

"I'm tryna see what that shit taste like. My money good."

"By the way, the call me Smoke. I run Harlem."

Young Money shook his hand. "Nice to meet you, bra, but look I got of eighth for you, and you don't owe me nothing."

"Aight, yo, datts wassup. How long you gon' be out here?"

"Shit till after the New Year's."

"Aight, look, son. Tap in, and if you ain't doing nothing, Club ——— gon' be popn'."

"I might slide through. Take my number down."

"What was all that about?" Mulan said.

"I just might found a play."

"Well, tell me more about that later."

"What's wrong with you?"

"Nothing, just a lil tired."

"We fenna get up out of here in a minute anyway. Ayy, Money," Young Money yelled his name. Money couldn't hear him. He was to busy breaking Stacy off on the dance floor. And Jay was getting a lap dance from Fendi. Chanele was in her own world on Instagram live. When Money finally came back to the VIP area, Young Money told them they was fenna get ready to leave. He called the hottest over and paid his tab. He gave her 38,000.

"So what y'all gon' do with the rest of the bottles that you didn't drink?"

"Do whatever you want with them."

Everybody walked out and got on the party bus. It was 2:00 a.m. Mulan was falling asleep in Young Money's arms. Once the party bus pulled up to the Trump Tower, everybody got off the bus and walked back to their suite. Young Money and Mulan went to their room as everybody else did. Chanele heard a light tap on her room door. As she cracked the door open, she couldn't believe who it was. "What you want?"

"I want you."

"Boy, you been acting like you couldn't speak all night," she said. He said to hisself. Money was admiring her beauty damn as she let him in. "Okay, I see somebody in their birthday suit."

"What is you talking about?"

"I'm talking bout you being ass whole naked."

"Boy, I'm always naked when I'm about to go to sleep, but wassup? Why is you in my room?"

"You know wassup," Money said as he tried to grab her ass. She slapped his hand away.

"Unhuggh, don't touch. You betta go rub on Stacy with all dat."

Money was tired of playing games, so he took charge. "Man, stop playing with me," he said as he started rubbing on her clit. He knew she was getting turned when she opened her legs and tilted her head back.

"Ooh shit, that feels so good. You fenna make me come." When

Chanele started moaning louder, he sped up. "Oh my god, I'm coming." After she finished coming, Money wiped his fingers off on the sheet after he did a smell check. He got up to leave, but before he could grab the doorknob, Chanele jumped off the bed. "Where the fuck you think you going?"

"I thought you wanted me to leave."

"Ha, you funny." She grabbed him by his Louis Vuitton belt and unbuckled his belt, slid his pants down, and gave him the best head he ever had. She was deep-throating him like she didn't have no gag reflexes as she put him to the back of her throat and held it there for several seconds.

"Damn, you deserve a trophy for this head." She looked him out her mouth and licked and sucked the tip of his head. She didn't want him to come yet, so she made a shove, and he was still rock-hard. Once she stopped, Money finally opened his eyes. "Why you stop?" and seen a pretty sight in front of him. Chanele was facedown, ass up. Money couldn't do nothing but smile as he took off his clothes.

As he got behind her, he slapped her on the ass. "Oow shit, do it again," she said and slapped the other ass cheek. As he slid inside her, her pussy instantly grabbed his dick. "Um, yes, give me that dick." Money started off with a long-stroke motion, and over her pussy started getting wetter. He spread up. "Ooow, that dick so good. Can I have it to myself?"

"Show me you want it all to yoself." Chanele started throwing her ass back as Money was standing tall all in her pussy.

"Oh, fuck, I'm fenna come. I'm coming." Money was fillen' hisself. He knew he put that dick up on her once she finished having her orgasm. Money pulled out and nutted on her back. Once he did that, he went to the bathroom and wiped off. As he was putting on his clothes, Chanele had asked him, "So what does this mean?"

"It mean whatever you want it to mean." With that being said, Money walked back to his room and got back in the bed with Stacy.

New Year's Day Club

—— was lit. Everybody had on the latest designer. Everybody was enjoying their self. It was ace of spade and D'usse bottles everywhere. Smoke was in the building with his people. "What's good, bra?"

"Shit, fam tryna get like you."

"Talk to me, I talk back. Look, yo, I'ma be straightforward with you. A nigga tryna get some of that sour desil. How much you tryna get."

"Like a hunned a month, so you can send me twenty-five a week."

"So let me ask you something, how much they are going for out here."

"They going for 3,500. The question is how much you gon' let um go for."

"I given to you for like 3,000."

"Say no more, young. Lock dat in."

After Young Money finished handling his business, he joined the party. "Everything good, bra," Money said.

"Yea, we looked in. We fenna really get to this bag. We gon' fall back off the licks for a minute in focus on this OT, Money."

"Fuck you niggas over here talking 'bout if a nickle bag is sold I need in," Jay said.

"Man, shut yo siked-out ass up. You know you in. I was just telln' Money I just locked us in with o boy."

"You think you can trust this nigga?" Jay replied.

"I don't know. We gon' see. Scary Money don't make no money. Let's go turn this bitch up. We gon' grab are bitches in go to the dance floor." Everybody was on the dance floor getn' it in. Chanele was twerkn' her ass all on Smoke, and Money was feeln' some type of way. "Ayy, let me holla at you for a minute," he said as he grabbed her by her arm. She shrugged away from him.

"Wassup, why you bugging because why is you all up on dat nigga like that? You don't even know him."

"Same reason why you all over dat bitch stay, so I'm doing me, in you do you," she said and walked off.

Stacy saw the whole thing. She made eye contact with Money and ran towards Chanele. "So wassup, bitch? You fucking my nigga?"

"I know this bitch ain't tryna come for me. Check this out, go ask yo nigga how this pussy feel. He should know. He was all in it the other night when you was sleep."

Stacy had heard enough. She grabbed Chanele by the hair and started upper-cutting her. Once Chanele came back to her senses, she started swinging like a wild woman, hitting Stacy with some lefts and rights to get that bitch sister beat that bitch ass. Fendi was yelling on the side. "Hey, break this shit up." The security guard came over, grabbing Chanele off Stacy. "Yea, bitch, that's why you got yo ass whipped," Chanele said.

"I'm sorry, y'all gotta go. We have zero tolerance for fighting in his club."

"Fuck this club. We going back to Cali anyway."

Young Money couldn't do nothing but shake his head with a grin on his face. "That shit is not funny. This some trifling-ass shit," Mulan said as she got up to leave.

The plane ride back was a quiet one; everybody was in their own thoughts. Mulan was lying on Young Money's shoulder as he was rubbing on her stomach. "Babe, yo stomach getting big."

"I know. I can't wait to find out what we have."

"I hope it's a girl. I mean, I just want to have a healthy baby. It doesn't matter if we have a girl or a boy," Young Money said.

Once the plane finally landed back at SFO Airport, everybody got off the plane, got their luggage, and went their separate ways. "All right, girl, call me when you get home," Mulan said to Fendi. Young Money and Mulan got in their car and drove home as Young Money got on the freeway. It was a lil traffic, so as they were waiting, Mulan all of a sudden got horny.

"Wassup? Why you looking at me like that?"

"No reason," she said, smiling at him as she reached inside his nice sweatpants, grabbing and massaging his penis up and down. Mulan had some soft hands, so that shit was feeln' hella good. As she was massaging his dick up and down she put her juicy lips on the tip of his dick, teasing him as she stopped. "Okay, I'm done."

"My nigga, stop playen' with me," he said as he lightly grabbed her by her hair, pushing her head down back towards his penis. This time, she put her whole mouth on him, licking his shaft up and down. She started deep-throating him. Young Money was stuck in a trance. "Babe, that shit feel hella good." As she deep-throated him several more times, Money busted a fat nut in Mulan's mouth, and she swallowed every last drip. Beep, beep. The car behind them was trying to get their attention to go. "Wooh shit, babe, what was that all about?"

"Just a lil something I've been wanting to do to you, and since I damn near been nauseated the whole time we was in New York, I had to bless you, but it's more where that came from once we get home."

"Well, since you put it like that, let me hurry up to get through this traffic."

Young Money was driving like a bat out of hell. "Boy, if you don't slow this car down 'fore you kill us," she said, laughing her nervousness off. Young Money made it home no less than five minutes. As they were walking through the door, they couldn't keep their hands off each other. They were tonguing each other down. As they made it to the bedroom,

Young Money stripped out his clothes, and Mulan followed suit. Mulan lay on the bed, and Young Money started kissing on her neck and sucked and licked both her nipples. As he was putting kisses down her stomach, she let out a light moan. As he reached her love box, he sucked and licked her clit like it was a juicy peach. "Ohh my god, babe, yes, right there. You gon' make me come. Oow, I love you so much."

"I love you too, babe," he said as he continued to make love to her clit. Mulan couldn't take it no more. She let outa loud cry fuck.

"I'm coming." Once she finished, she got up and grabbed Young Money dick and put it right in here mouth and was sucking the tip of his dick, then put inch by inch in her mouth all the way to the back of her throat until she started choking. Young Money wanted to be inside her, so he pushed her down and slid in her missionary style. Mulan's pussy was so wet and tight.

"Damn, babe, this pussy so good fuck."

"Yes, baby, this all yours. This yo pussy. Oow shit, I'm coming." Young Money kept beating her pussy up, then he bent her over and started fucking her doggy style. He slapped her on the ass. As she started throwing her ass back, Mulan was putting that pussy on him. They both came at the same time and fell in each other's arms. "We just got it in," Mulan said as she was lying in Young Money's arms.

"Man, we definitely did," he said wit one eye open.

"Ayy, babe, my mom wants to meet you. I told her about you, and I also told her you was pregnant."

"You did? What she say?"

"She was trippin' at first, and then I told her about you, and she wanna get to know you, so we gon' go over there this Sunday. You heard me, babe." Young Money looked to his left, and Mulan was necked out he couldn't do nothing but laugh as he closed his eyes and followed right behind her.

"Ayy, bra, we dem niggas. We got that bag. We 'bout that murder game in all the bitches on us, Jay said as he and Money were parked on Oakdale, sitn' in the car, smoking on some cooks. "Yea, that shit sound good, but pass the wood, my nigga."

"Jay, hit it one more time in past it. So, Money, bra, what was that shit about wit Chanele?"

"All, boy." Money let out a slight chuckle. "Let me tell you what happened. You remember when we came back from the club the day of my b-day. I waited for my bitch to go to sleep. I crept to Chanele's room. But tell me why she was tryna play hard to get." He hit the wood and passed it back to Jay. "So when I knocked on the door, she was tryna act like she wasn't go let me in, so I pushed through the door."

"Damn, bra, so you was gon' just take the pussy."

"Nah, never. That you know. I had her begging for it, in you know I did my thang."

"That's why she was all in her feeling."

"So let me ask you this, you gon' double back."

Money couldn't do nothing but smile. "I might but baby gotta chill with that extra shit tryna fight my bitch in shit."

"Man, you already know that come wit it," Jay said. "Wassup though, you tryna go on one, I'm tryna catch one," Jay said.

"You already know I'm 'bout dat drill," Money replied.

"Were you tryna go though."

"Let's go pick on them wood niggas. We gon' walk through Shorview in go through Lasalle."

"Bra, fuck all that," Money said. "That's hella walking, my nigga. We just gon' park by Young Blood Park in go through the park, in if we catch som'thing, we just gon' come back to the car."

"Aight." Money and Jay pulled off. Once they pulled up to Young Blood Park, they got out the car and walked through the park and hit the fence. As they were walking up Kirkwood, there was some body walking down the street.

Money whispered to Jay, "Ayy, you see dat nigga walking towards us? We gon' come from behind this car. Shoot first, ask questions later."

Once the opp got closer, Money and Jay came from behind, the car guns blazing bloc bloc bloc bloc bloc bloc bloc bloc. The opp got hit all in the face in the torsle. After they seen he wasn't moving no more, they took off running back toward the car. As they got in the car, they pulled off and slowly went through West Point, slid all the way down third, and got on the Baybrige. "We just got all over that nigga," Jay said.

"We deffinitely did. You should of seen dat nigga face when we came from around the car. You would of sweam he saw the gran reapper in where you going anyway. To my bitch house."

"Who?"

"I mean, I don't even know why I said that. We all know Fendi got that a wiped," Money said, laughing.

"Yea, whatever, nigga but wassup with that doe Pedro owe us?"

"I don't know. We gon' holla at Young Money tomorrow because I'm tryna go see wassup wit Johnny. I'm fenna go bust down the whole grill, in I'm tryna bust down a new rolly," Money said.

"Okay, I see you, boy. I'm fenna bust my shit down too. All niggas tryna copy niggas in shit pussy at knowbody copying you in coming, bost down to." As Jay was pulling up to Fendi's spot he FaceTimed her.

"Hello," she said in a groggy voice.

"Babe, open the door."

"Aight," she said and hung up the phone. Money and Jay walked in the house.

"Wassup, sis."

"Hi, Money, damn, wassup with the attitude."

"Boy, bye," Fendi said and walked off. Jay followed suit and went with Fendi. To the room. Chanele was a light sleeper; she knew she heard some voice, so she got up and walked to the kitchen in her boy shorts and a tank top. As she walked in the kitchen, she poured herself some Minute Maid.

"Duke, wassup, Chanele," Money said, wrapping his arms around her. He made her jump not because of his arms wrapped around her. They actually felt good. But she had to remember that she wasn't fucking with him.

"Uh huh, watch out," she said as she wiggled out his embrace.

"Damn, my nigga, that's you acting."

"Share is especially how you fronted on me in New York. You got me fucked up." As she was talking, Money kissed her, and the spark was lit from there. They started kissing passionately all the way to her room. As Money leaned on the bed, she stratled him, kissing on his neck. As she took off his shirt, she put wet soft kisses down his chest. Money was wiggling out his pants. As she reached for his dick that was already semihard from the foreplay, she wrapped her mouth around his love pole and started sucking and licking. Once she found her rhythm, she started deep-throating him. Once she knew he was rock-hard, she climbed on top and inserted his love pole and started moving her hips back and forth. "Oow, this dick good. You bet not give my dick to nobody," she said as she was riding him with her head tilted back. "Fuck, I'm fenna come. Oow shit, I'm coming."

"That's what I'm talking 'bout making that pussy cum for me," Money said. As Chanele was having multiple orgasm, she wasn't done yet, so she got off Money's love pole and got on all fours. As Money was fenna penetrate her, she started wiggling her ass. That shit turned Money on, so he slapped her on the ass, which aroused Chanele to let out a light moan. When Money finally put his love pole inside Chanele's wet tight pussy, she let out a loud moan.

"Huggh, yes, just like that. Beat this pussy up, Daddy. Yes, you fenna make me come again." Money was going hard, gripping both ass cheeks, then letting off a heavy load inside Chanele. They both were out of breath. As they lay down, Chanelle was lying down on Money's chest. "I can't keep doing this. Like don't get me wrong, the sex is everything, but I need more than that. I mean, I'm not tripping off yo lil girlfriend. I just want to be able to spend some quality time with you. I think I'm falling in love with you. Money, did you hear me?"

"Um huh," he said as he was dozing off. "I got you. We gon' do as I promise."

"Yeah, we gon' see because I'm not fucking playing with you," she said as she let her eyes close.

Young Money woke up and went to the bathroom to go take a piss. After he was finished, he turned on the Channel 2 news. "Last night, it was the first murder of this new year. A man in his sixties was shot multiple times. They say they were trying to figure out with the motive that nobody seen the suspects. Back to you, John."

"Damn, that's crazy. Somebody killed a dope feind. Mutherfucka shouldn't been outside anyway," he said as he FaceTimed Money. Ring, ring, ring. "Wassup, my nigga, wake yo game up."

"Bra, why is you calling me so early? You on some tweaker shit?"

"You ain't know the early bird get the worm first."

"You do look like one of them pigeons that be in the hood."

"Fuck you, nigga, in who you laid up with my nigga."

"Oh, this baby. I'm baby now," Chanele said. "You definetly is shit the way you put it on a nigga you gone be wifey."

"Boy, don't be talking like that because you is not ready for all that."

"Yeah, I hear you, ayy, YM, wassup though. You fucking up my early Money pussy."

"I was just tapn' in. Do yea some og nigga got smacked last night on the wood."

"What? Fa real, my nigga," Money said with a smirk on his face. "That's crazy. Niggas be doing anything."

"Aight, bra, kick rocks when you nigga going to the city."

"What you mean niggas."

"Bra, you wit Jay. I already know wassup," Young Money said as he hung up.

"You hungry," Chanele asked Money.

"You know I'm hungry."

"All right, I'm fenna go make some breakfast."

"Where yall bathroom at?"

"Down the hall to the right, not the left."

"Why you say it like that?"

"Because the room on the left is my sister."

"Man, ain't nobody gon' go in her room." Money got up and went to the bathroom. As he was walking down the hall, he opened the door on the left on purpose. As he opened the door, he seen Fendi riding Jay reverse cowgirl style.

"Oow, Jay, I love this dick." Fendi saw Money watching, and that turned her on even more. Money saw that she didn't stop, so he closed the door. As he finished using the bathroom, he walked back to Chanele's room.

"Dang, boy, what took you so long? The food ready."

Chanele went to get his plate. After Money finished eating, he got dressed. "So when I'ma get to see you again?" Money said.

"I don't know. Matter of fact, it's this movie that's coming out Friday. You can take me to go see it."

"So what? This a date we going on?"

Money said, "Something like that."

"Aight, it's a date then. I'ma tap in." He gave her a hug and left.

Young Money was bending a few comers when TaTa was FaceTiming him. "Wassup wit yo, phoney ass?" she said.

"Why I gotta be all dat?" he said with a smile on his face.

"Because, my nigga, you been acting real brand-new every since you got that bitch pregnet."

"Watch yo mouth, bitch."

"See, that's what I'm talking 'bout. You even taking up for her."

"TaTa, what the fuck you want? This is what you called me for? To fuck up my day."

"Boy, shut up. I called you because I was thinking 'bout you, and I want to see you."

"Aight, I'ma pull up on you."

"Don't just be telln' me anything."

"My nigga, I'ma call you."

"Aight, lil ugly," she said with a wide smile on her face.

As Young Money was turning into Oakdale, he saw Money bending a left coming into Oakdale as well. Honk, honk. Money came to a stop. "Wassup, bra, what's pop'n'?" Money said.

"Shit, you know me surfn'. Ayy, you seen the news."

"Wah, what happened?"

"They said some OG nigga got smacked on the wood."

"What? For real blood ha ha ha. That's fucked up. Niggas ain't shit. Ayy, though, I gotta holla at you, bra," Money said. "Pull up to Mom's house."

They both parked side by side. Once they got out the car, they walked up the stairs. Young Money and Money went to their rooms to go put they guns up. "So wassup, my nigga. What you got on yo mind?"

"When I tell you" you can't be bustin' no funny."

"Man, tell me, my nigga, for I start getting on that p-nut head."

"Aight, look, you know how the news said it was a OG nigga that got killed on the wood. That was me in Jay."

Young Money fell out laughing. "Bra, tell me that wasn't yall. Ha ha ha you niggas killed a dude. I'm on you niggas."

"My nigga, we thought we had one. We was all over that nigga. O yea, I bet y'all was all the wanted was some cream ha ha ha." Young Money got up to leave. "Where you going, bra?"

"Fenna go check some heed from TaTa, only you niggas gotta redeem yallself," he said as he left out. Money was left with his thoughts. He couldn't believe how Young Money laughed at him. He was in competition with Young Money ever since they was younger. It wasn't envy; it was just they both were competitive when it came to each other. Money left out the house and walked through the projects. As he was walking up the B to go to Danyale house, DD[2] was coming out the cuts. "Wassup, Young Money."

"This ain't Young Money. This Money, big bra."

"Damn, lil bra. Y'all lil niggas look just alike."

"We is twins."

"Nigga, I know, but wassup though? Why you walking around this bitch like you lost yo best friend."

Money was silent for several seconds, then he spoke up. "I'ma keep it real, big bra. I'm tryna get a body. That's all, my nigga. That shit ain't nothing. That's a layup when you tryna bust yo move."

"Shit, whenever you ready."

"Aight, we gon' bust are move in like a hour."

"Its still early."

"I know this the best time. When everybody come outside, meet me back right here in a hour." DD^2 slid back in the cut, and Money walked across the street to Danyale's house.

Knock, knock. "Who is it?" Danyale said as she opened the door.

"Wassup, stranger, haven't heard from you in a while."

"I been busy."

"Busy doing what? Being a hoe."

"Watch yo mouth in you talkin' 'bout hoe bitch, Yo baby daddy been over here anyway."

"Oh, I can't hear you. The cat got your tongue."

"What are you talkin' 'bout? He was just over here spending time with his kids."

"Yea, I hear yo," Money said as he walked in the house. High Money, Danyale's daughter, ran and jumped in his arms.

"Wassup, Dooty, what you been up to?"

"Nothing."

"You been being good?"

"Yea."

"Aight, I'ma take you to the candy house, in you can get whatever you want," she said as she wiggled out his arms. Money went to go sit on the couch. "Babe, you hungry."

"Nah, I'm good. I'ma just put you a plate up for later, and what's wrong with you? You ain't never turned down my food."

"I just got a lot on my mind right now."

"Well, I know how to fix that," she said as she walked towards the couch and sat next towards him. She started kissing on his neck. As she tried to reach in his pants, he stopped her.

"What you doing? Don't you see lil Money in here playing?" She smacked her teeth.

"Jazzmine, yo play in yo room."

"Why, Mom? I'm playing right here."

"Lil girl, what the fuck I say? Take yo lil ass to yo room." Once she went to her room, Danyale continued where she left off. She unbuckled Money's belt and pulled his dick out and started rubbing it up and down. Once she put her mouth on it, Money leaned his head back. It seemed like once she put her mouth on him, all the tension left his body. As she started deep-throating him, Money grabbed her by her ponytail and started fucking her mouth. As he was fucking her mouth, she was gagging and choking, but all that shit was turning her on. Once she stopped, she slid her face see-through boy shorts to the side. She sat on top of him and started riding him. Oow, Money, this dick so good. Yes, Daddy, I love this dick."

"You love this dick you gon' come on this dick."

"Yes, o my god. Oow, I'm fenna come, Money. I'm coming." As Danyale came, Money lifted her off him and put his dick in her mouth. As Danyale was sucking and licking, he let out a heavy load in her mouth. She swallowed every drop.

"Damn, babe, you took a nigga soul out his body."

"You know I had to get you right."

"You definitely got me right," he said as he walked to the bathroom to wash off. When he came out the bathroom, he walked in the kitchen, opened up the refrigerator, and grabbed the Minute Maid juice in the water fountain.

"Un huh, what I tell you about drinking my kids shut."

"Oh, my bad," he said with a light chuckle. "You coming back later."

"Yeah, I be back, but look, go grab my blower out the room."

"What you need that for?"

"Man, go get my shit, my nigga."

Once she went to go get it, Money was in deep thought. "Huh, you better be careful."

"Don't trip. I'ma be good," he said and headed outside.

As he was walking down the street, DD^2 was walking out the cut. "Wassup, lil bra, you ready?"

"I stay ready. Let me see what you rockin wit," DD^2 said. Money pulled out an FN.

"Okay, I see you."

"What you rockin wit, big bra."

DD^2 lifted up his hoodie, showing a mini M-16 with a vest on. "So look, lil bra. Just follow my league. We gon' go through the back in come out at the top of Oakdale, than we gon' cut through the Newpark, cut through the stairs that take you to the middle of the G. Whoever we see we getting on and the same way we came, that's how we leaving, so keep up."

As they was fenna walk off, Black and White drove down Oakdale; they was SFPD. DD^2 and Money continued on their walk. As they got closer to the G, Money put one in the head. They both were in killer mode. Once they were walking up the stairs, DD^2 saw two niggas chillen' in a car behind tint. "A, lil bra, you see them niggas in the whip thinking they under behind that were right there in that gray Benz."

"Yea, I see them niggas they lackn' right now."

"I'ma get the driver. You get the passenger." Boom boom boom boom boom boom chop chop chop chop chop click click. Once they saw both bodies weren't moving, they took off running. As they made it back to Oakdale, they tucked their guns in and went their separate ways.

"A, lil bra, you did yo shit, and that was dem suckas. I been tryna get I'ma fenna go Smoke to this," DD^2 said.

"Me too spent off in slid through the back door of Danyale apartment. Aghhh, boy, you scared the fuck out of me."

"Oh, my bad, babe," he said as he started closing the blinds. "That's a damn shame. Let me find out that was you. I don't know what you talking 'bout. but if anybody come over here looking for me, I ain't here."

"Yea, I hear you," she said. Money walked off and went to the room.

Young Money was getting some head from TaTa when he heard shots fired. TaTa stopped sucking. "You heard that."

"Yea, I did," he said as he guided her head back towards his dick. He laid his head back as her mouth wrapped around his dick. Once he busted a fat nut in her mouth, he got up to leave.

"Damn, a bitch can't get no dick."

"I got you. Don't trip. I'ma pull up on you later."

"I swear I can't fucking stand you. You always frontin' on me."

"But it's good though. I'ma give this pussy to somebody else."

"Bitch, I don't care. It ain't like you ain't been throwing that pussy a party."

"See, I knew you don't care about me," she said as tears were coming out her eyes.

"Man, bitch, you siked out," he said and walked out the house. He tried to FaceTime Money, but he didn't get no answer, so he hopped in the car and drove to the house.

Once he got in the house, his mom was sitting on the couch. "Hi, son, come give Moma a hug."

"Wassup, Ma, what you got going on?"

"Oh, nothing. Got some neck bones, cabbage macaroni and cheese, and some corn bread cooking."

"Okay." Ma hooked it up, then he said as he sat beside her, "Ayy, Ma."

"What, Young Money?"

"You ever thought about moving from right here."

"Why do I need to move? I've been living here my whole life. I'm perfectly fine where I'm at, and whatever happened on you bringing that girl BF?"

"Her name is Mulan, Mom."

"Well, hell, I don't you have so many of them lil heffas. You need to settle down with Mulan then."

"I know, Ma," he said as he got up to walk to his room.

"In don't be going nowhere the food is gone. Be done in a minute in call yo brother in tell him to come home in eat."

"Aight, Ma, anything else?"

"Yea, and I need some money, so all right, that."

Young Money couldn't do anything but smile. Once he got in his room, he put his blower up, went to his safe, grabbed a few stacks out, looked at his stash and smiled. "Damn, we really getting Money," he said to no one in particular. As he was lying on his bed, his phone started ringing. "Wassup, bra, where you at? Mom's cooked, so bring yo big head ass to the spot."

Beep. "Hold on, bra. This that nigga Jay."

"What's poppn'?"

"Shit at the house."

"Aight, I'm fenna pull up on you," Jay said. Young Money hung up.

Money came walking in the house. "Wassup, Ma?"

"Hey, son, where you coming from?"

"Up the street."

"You betta be careful out there. I heard some gun shots earlier."

"I'm good, Ma. Young Money in the back."

"Yea, he back there."

"Damn, my nigga, you don't know how to knock. I could of been fucking yo bitch."

"Nigga, if you was fucking my bitch, she was never my bitch."

"Yea, I hear you, my nigga," Young Money said. "Ayy, Money, let me find out that was yo crazy ass that pulled that drill."

"I don't know what you talking 'bout," Money said with a smirk on this face. "Why you looking at me like that weird-ass nigga."

"Because, my nigga, I know you."

"Nah, that was definitely me, bra."

"What was definitely you?" Jay said as he walked in. "What the fuck you niggas in here whispering about?"

"He was fenna tell me before yo big head ass came interrupting."

"Well, proceed."

"Man, you niggas siked out. It ain't nothing to really know me, in big bra did are theng. We crept on them niggas on the g. I dropped the whole clip out the FN, and we got on."

"So that's where you went. Why you didn't tell me?"

"Because that shit happened on some fluke shit."

"Yea, yea, nigga good for you. You got a body, but wassup, Young Money. Wassup with that play in New York."

"Jay sand shit. I just gotta tap in, and we gon' be good he talking a hunned a week, so we gon' run it up matter of fact. I'ma tap in wit um right now. Young Money, text Smoke. Wassup, bra? What's poppn'? Wassup yo? When you gon' pull up on me."

"I'ma holla at my boy and I'ma get back at you."

"Aight, yo get at me."

"So look, this the play. We need to find a conect who can let us buy in bulk," Young Money said.

"Ayy, remember White Boy Mike? The one we went to school wit?" Jay replied.

"Yea, what about him?" Money answered.

"That nigga be on the gram showing hella pounds. I mean, we all know it's his dad shit. I'ma get at him and see wassup."

"Well, you do that, and you know what else you niggas can do? Y'all can get the fuck out my room, dry-ass niggas. I got some bunz coming." Jay and Money were headed outside after Money changed his clothes.

"Money, where you think you going? The food fenna be ready," his mom said.

"Ma, just put my plate up. I'ma be back in a minute."

"Always running them damn streets." She couldn't do anything but shake her head.

"So look, Jay, call ya boy so we can lock them as a matter of fact. Let's pull up on me."

"Hold up. Let me call him first." Ring, ring, ring. "Wassup, brought, what's been going on?" Jay said.

"Shit, dude, you knew growing this pot and getting stoned."

"O yea, ayy, check it out. I'm tryna holla at you 'bout some business."

"You know where I'm at. Come on up."

White Boy Mike stayed in Humboldt County, which was where everybody grew weed. "Aight, I'ma be out there tomorrow."

"In, Jay, come by yoself."

"Aight, it's good." Once he hung up, he looked at Money.

"So what's the play?" Money said.

"I'm gon' holla at 'em tomorrow."

"I'm coming with you."

"That's what I was gon' talk to you about. He just want me to come."

"Okay, that's cool." Money was feeling some type of way because he couldn't come. "So look, bra, Chanele in Fendi tryna go out Friday. You fucken' wit it."

"I might. Wassup, though, let's go get some tree, and I ain't tryna go to that nigga slim. He been having boof lately. Let's go to the Cannabis Club." Before they pulled off, Money went to go grab his blower.

Mulan was at home lying in her bed when she seen Young Money FaceTiming her. She picked up on the first ring. "Wassup, babe, what you doing?"

"Nothing, missing you, and besides cramping, I'm good."

"What I was gon' say, you tryna come to my mom house? She cooking, and I want you to meet her."

"Okay, I be there in a minute."

"All right, baby moma. I see you in a minute."

After Mulan hung up, she called Chanele. Ring, ring. "Wassup, cuzz, what you doing?" Mulan said.

"Minding my business and staying out of yours."

"Damn, why the shade?"

"Because you phony. I ain't seen you in forever. Ever since you got pregnant, you've been acting brand-new."

"Girl gone with that shit. Anyway, I was gonna ask you what should I wear. Young Money asked me to come to his house. His mom wants to meet me."

"Girl, ain't you pregnant? You betta put on a Vicki sweatsuit and call it a day."

"That is so trifling. I don't even know why I even called you. You are no help."

"Well, figure it out yoself because I don't know what to tell you."

"Bye, girl, I know what I'm aware." Once Mulan got off the phone, she went through her closet, and as she was scanning through it, she saw a Dolce & Gabbana outfit she hadn't worn yet. So she grabbed it and went to go get in the shower after she got dressed. She looked at herself in her closet mirror. Once she saw she was on point, she headed out the door. Ring, ring. "Baby Zaddy, what you doing?"

"Why you sound hella ghetto?"

"I thought that's how you like them."

"How you figured that?"

"Because I be seeing that one lil bitch on the gram with yo name in her mouth, and she be sounding hella rachet."

"My nigga, what bitch you talkin' 'bout?"

"You know what bitch I'm talking 'bout. Her name Talicious on Instagram."

"Talicious? I don't even know her."

"Yea, whatever, nigga. Just know when I have this baby, I'm coming for dat bitch straight up, and I was calling to tell you I'm on my way. I'm crossing the bridge right now. I call you when I'm outside." *This nigga think he slick. I don't know why he even lying like I'm some dumb bitch*, she said to herself. As she pulled up to Young Money's house, she called him. Ring, ring. "I'm outside," she said and hung up. Young Money came outside to meet Mulan.

"Wassup, babe," he said as he gave her a hug.

"Damn, I don't get no kiss."

"Nope, I'm not feeling you right now," as they got inside the house.

Once they got in the house, Mulan greeted Young Money's mom. "Hi, Mom," she said as she gave her a big hug. "Mom, this Mulan, the girl I been telling you about."

"I know who she is, boy. You been talking 'bout her since she been on her way over here." Mulan looked at Young Money and smiled. She noted to herself that she could be nice to him because of the attitude she had when she got there. Young Money went to his room to go roll up some cookies. "So, Mulan, what do you see in my son Young Money?"

"Well, I see everything in him. He means the world to me. Since the day we met, we have been inseparable. I feel like he have my best interest at heart, and I have his." Little did she know Mulan was one of the main reasons for Young Money's success. "He also protects me, and I feel safe with him. That's my soul mate."

Money came walking in. "Okay, Ma, it smells good in here."

Young Money's mom and Mulan's convo got cut short. "We gon' finish this talk later. Let me go get these plates ready." Money went to his room. As he was 'bout to walk in, Young Money stuck his head out his room door.

"What's poppin, my nigga, where you been at?"

"At ya bitch's house, nigga, and she had some grade A head. The bitch should of went to Stanford." They both had to laugh at that one.

"Speaking of bitches," Young Money had a serious look on his face look, "bra, that bitch TaTa on her way over here. I need you to make sure she don't make it to the spot."

Money couldn't do nothing but shake his head. "I gotta holla at you about something too," Money said.

"Aight, nigga, tell me when you get back."

As Money was walking down the stairs, he saw TaTa walking towards the house. "Wassup wit TaTa."

"Wassup, Money? Where yo big head ass brother at?"

"He busting a move right now, and my mom in there sleep, so don't nobody got time for that loud ass shit you be on."

"Okay, that's fine, but let me tell you what I think because y'all two be playing games. First of all, I see dat nigga car right there, so I know he in the house, but it's good. Joke's on him."

"What that 'pose to mean?"

"He gon' find out once he come out that house and find his windows bust out."

"You wild, Ta, but I'ma get at you."

As they both went their separate ways, Money was walking back towards the house. As he was walking, he saw that same black car. He meant to tell Young Money. About within a split second, shots were fired. Bloc, bloc, bloc, bloc, bloc. As the car sped off, everything slowed down. Money was on the ground as his life flashed before his eyes. TaTa ran towards Money to give him some support. "Hold on, Money. It's going to be okay. I called the ambulance, so just breathe slow and don't panic." Young Money, Mulan, and Young Money's mom came running out the house. What Money saw next brought tears to his eyes; he ran to his brother's side.

"Ta, what happened?"

"I don't know. I mean, we was talking, and next thing you knew, Money was walking back towards the house, and a all black car pulled up. Everything happened so fast."

"Fuck," Young Money said. "Bra, you aight? You know who ever did this, they gon' pay for this shit."

As Money was tryna talk, he started coughing up blood. That only made Young Money more mad. The ambulance came and took Money to the hospital. Once everything started to settle in, TaTa was thinking to herself, *Who is this bitch all by moma Money?* "So this what you been doing playing house with this bitch while I'm out here saving Money life?"

"TaTa, don't start that shit right now," Young Money said.

"Nah, please start," Mulan said. "Because this bitch about to get her ass beat."

"Bitch, I got yo, bitch, you must don't know about me," TaTa said.

"Trust and believe I got the tea on you. You ain't even doing nothing, lil girl, and to let you know I'm fenna have his baby, checkmate." As Young Money was holding Mulan back, TaTa looked at Young Money.

"So is this true, Young Money?" He couldn't do nothing but look at her. The odd silence gave her the answer she was looking for. Mulan was loving every moment. TaTa walked off with tears in her eyes. Young Money walked off towards the house; he had one thing on his mind, and that was murder. He grabbed his Geezy and got in the car. As Money sped off, Mulan tried to run after him. "Come here, baby." Mulan went to lay her head on Young Money mom's shoulder. "It's gonna be all right, baby. Everything gon' be all right." They both couldn't hold back the tears. Once they arrived at General Hospital, Money mom checked in at the trauma unit.

"Hi, mam, how may I help you?"

"Ahh, yes, I'm looking for Money Johnson."

"Ahh, hold on one sec," the nurse tech said.

"Okay, mam, he's in room 133 on the second floor, and who may you be? They're only letting immediate family members in."

"I'm his mother."

"Okay, perfect, you cleared to go in. Who may you be?" Young Money's mom spoke up for her.

"She's family, uh well, okay, I'll just put her down as the sister." They walked towards the elevator to go where Money was at. "Hi, mam, how may I help you?"

"Yes, I'm looking for Money Johnson. I'm his mother."

"Okay, one moment. I'll go get the doctor." As the doctor was approaching, Money's mom was holding her breath, anticipating her son's fate.

The doctor took off his gloves and raised his mask down. "Hi, ma'am, who might you be?"

"High, I'm Money's mom. How is he?"

"Well, mam, I got some good news."

Money mom couldn't do nothing but exhale as all her worries went out the window. "Thank you, Doctor. Thank you so much."

"Don't thank me. Thank my team. They're the ones who took care of business. I might say we have one of the best surgeons in California. Well, let me let you see him. He's in stable condition. The bullet went through his lower abdomen, so he's heavily sedated, but he's talking." As she walked in the door, she couldn't do nothing but smile. She was so happy her baby was okay. Once she got by his bed, she grabbed his hand.

Young Money was sliding around smoking on a fat wood slapping. *Man, this shit crazy*, he was thinking too his self. *How the fuck this shit happen at the spot right at the spot, my nigga? I'm tellen' you I'm definitely on shit, my fucking brother. I'm getting on whoever had something to do with this.* As his phone started ringing, he was distracted from his train of thoughts. He saw it was Jay calling.

"Wassup, my nigga, why I seen some many shit on da gram? Tell me dat shit ain't true," Jay said.

"Bra, you already know how I'm playing it. I'm fenna do my shit though you stay ot. I'ma hold it down out there."

"We still gotta get this, Money. We gotta talk too when you touch down."

"Aight, but look though, is bra aight?"

"Yeah, dat nigga good. He had a flesh woon in and out."

"Okay, that's wassup. As long as he's good, I'ma tap in when I finish getting it in," Jay replied.

"Aight, my nigga, I'm fenna get in traffic."

Once Young Money got back in traffic, he turned the music back up, smoking on some runts. He picked up his phone and dialed TaTa. Ring, ring. "Hello."

"Wassup? What you doing?"

"I'm at home. Why?"

"I'm fenna come get you."

"Yeah, I hear you." Young Money hung up the phone and headed back to the projects. As Young Money pulled up to the hood, he slid back to the house to go change his clothes and hop in the shower. Once he got in the shower, he let the water hit his face. He was thinking how fast his life changed. He was just graduating high school with no money. Here it is. He nineteen now. He got everything he ever wanted. He had over almost 500,000,000. He did the math. Her made all that money within months, not including the money they was fenna get from OT. Everything was good. He was getting money, fenna have a baby. Everything was looking good, but he still was missing his cuzzin Shota. He was beefn' with hella niggas all over his cuzzin, not to mention his brother was in the hospital. He hopped out the shower, lotioned up through some Gucci cologne, and then got dressed. Once he finished getting dressed, he went to his safe, opened it, grabbed some money, and then he grabbed his blower. Once he got back in the car, he pulled up to TaTa's house. Ring, ring, ring. "Wassup, come outside."

"Oh, okay, I'm 'pose to just jump when you say jump."

"My niggah, why is you playing wit me? Here I come right now," TaTa said.

Once she got in the car, she had attitude all over her face. Young Money slid off. He felt the tension coming from TaTa. "So you ain't got nothing to say?" she said.

"I mean, ain't much to say. I'm fenna have a baby and me in Mulan together."

TaTa couldn't hold back her tears. "So why you fucking come get me, then huh to tell me some shit like? This like I been fucking with you since day one."

"My nigga, you act like . . . you know what, I ain't even fenna go there with you, my nigga, but look, check it out. When you was out there talking to my brother, what happened and tell me everything you saw?"

TaTa wiped her eyes. "You know what, I'ma tell you what you need to know since that's all you care about."

"Bitch, what the fuck you mean since that's all I care about? I'm tryna see who the fuck shot my brother, and, bitch, you was there."

"So what are you tryna say so? You think I had something to do with this."

"You know what, I ain't even fenna go there with you. It's good. I see you done changed. You let that bitch change you."

"Man, fuck all that. What car them niggas was in that shot my brother?" Young Money said.

"I think them niggas were in a BMW. It was all black."

"What kind of BMW?"

"It was small one." Young Money was thinking about what TaTa just had said. He played back what she said. They was in a small BMW. Niggas don't even drive them. He slid to twin. He parked the car, and he looked at TaTa.

"Look, blood, I know you ain't fillen' how shit played out. I didn't want you to find out like this. I'ma just keep it straight a hunned. You already know I fuck wit you the long way. I just can't make you my main bitch, you know that. And why the fuck is that you for every body. That's why, bitch."

"I ain't never for everybody, so don't ever try to come for me. I don't even fuck with niggas. I be in my own lane doing me."

"Yeah, I hear you," Young Money said.

"So do you love her?" TaTa said.

Several seconds passed, then Young Money gave her the answer she was looking for. "Yeah, I love her. She fenna have my baby."

"Oh, I know. I was there when what's her name told me."

"Do you love me, Young Money?"

"Yeah, I got love for you."

"That's not what I was looking for, but I take it. It's whatever I told you about what happened. Can you drop me off now?" As Young Money was driving back to the hood, Mulan was calling.

"Wassup, babe"

"Oh, nothing, still at the hospital with your mom. They were changing your brother bandages. I miss you. I want you to rub my stomach."

"Oh yeah, you know I can't wait to rub on yo stomach. I'ma put kisses all over it."

"We gon' see when we get home," Mulan said.

"Okay, babe, just hit me. Yo mom staying here at the hospital. I'm fenna go home in a minute. I call you when I get there."

"Aight, hit me."

"Love you."

"Love you too," Young Money said as he hung up. When TaTa heard him say them words to another female, it hurt her even more; a tear ran down her face. Once Young Money pulled up to the projects, he went to go drop TaTa off.

As he got back in traffic, he slid through a few hoods he had beef wit. "Damn, where these niggas at usually it would of been niggas outside out of all days." He couldn't catch nothing, so he slid back to the hood. Once he got there, he parked his car, and he got out. As he was walking, he saw his big bra DD^2. "Wassup, lil bra? I heard what happened to lil bra. He good?"

"Yea, he had a lil flesh wound. I just came from sliding. Ain't none of them suckas outside. Usually they would of been outside after pulling some shit like this."

"Look, lil bra, you been doing hella shit. You gotta pay attention to who wants to see you dead, and you can't even answer that because you got problems with a few people. So who you think it was?"

"Me personally, I'm not tryna be all in yo business, but I've been watching you, and you been doing yo thang, and I'm proud of you." What was just said meant a lot to Young Money. He always wanted acknowledgment from DD^2. "But yeah, lil bra, you gotta keep yo eyes open and them Asians be serious about their money too." Young Money looked at DD^2 with that "how the fuck you know about that like I told you I got" eyes everywhere. Young Money looked to his right, and once he looked to his left, DD^2 was gone. *Fuck, why this nigga always doing this shit?* You would have thought this nigga was a ghost. After talking to DD^2, Young Money had a lot to think about.

Money woke up in the hospital not knowing where he was at. From the prior events that took place, he remembered talking to TaTa, and the next thing he knew, an all-black BMW slid by him with the window down, and next thing he knew, shots were fired, and he seen a China boy who was the shooter. As shit started making sense, he knew what time it was. When his thoughts stopped running through his head, he seen Danyale in one corner, and his mom was still by his side. As he came too, Danyale came to his bedside. "Hey, baby, you scared us. Me in the kids was worried about you." Money's mom thought to herself, *Is what she mean us them badass kids, and I do not like her she is too old for my baby, but I'ma act like I like her for now.* "Wassup, Mom."

"Hey, baby."

"You all right?"

"Yeah, I'm good, just a lil thirsty. Can you get me a Sprite, and where Young Money?"

"He's on his way. Let me go get you that Sprite." As Money's mom went to get his Sprite, Danyale came to his bedside.

"Wassup, babe, I was so scared of losing you. I don't know what I would have done if I were to lose you."

"I'm good. Stop crying. The doc said it was just a flesh wound. Come here and give me a kiss." As Danyale was giving Money a kiss, Stacy was walking in with Money's mom.

"Ugh, umm." Stacy had cleaned his thought like she had something blocking her airways. She did that just to make her presence known. When Danyale turned around, she saw some lil girl looking like she was fresh out of high school.

"Uhm, who is you?" Stacy said.

"I think Money can answer that question for you," Danyale said. They both looked at Money. There was an awkward silence in the room.

"Yeah, Money, so who is this bitch?" Stacy said.

"Man, y'all chill out," he said with a light chuckle. "My mom's in here, in y'all doing hella shit."

"Don't mind me. I'm not even here right now."

"As you know, Money mom didn't like Danyale for all the reasons she had. Look, Money, I see you got hella shit going on, and I'm not the one to disrespect someone's mother. Hit me when you get ready." After she said that, she walked off but not before she said her last little words to Stacy. "Check this out, you lil bitch, before you ever call me out my name, make sure you put Ms. Bitch before it, and before you come for me, make sure you do your homework because I beat lil girls' asses for fun." Before Stacy could reply, Danyale was already walking out the door. Stacy had an attitude all over her face.

"Why you looking like that?" Money said.

"Boy, you know wassup. Why was that bitch all in yo face like that like she was fenna kiss you?"

"Man, that wasn't nothing. That's somebody from the hood, me in her friends."

"Oh yeah, y'all friends let me find out you fucking that bitch, it's gon' be a problem. Excuse my language, Ms. Money, but yo son be driving me crazy."

"Girl, I know his ass a headache."

"Young Money came walking in. "Wassup, bra? I see you finally came out yo slumber."

"Man, tell me about it. They had me doped up. I need some more of dat shit." Money chuckled.

"What you need to do is get up out of this bed so we can handle," Young Money said.

"The doctor said he would be getting released today," replied Ms. Money. "Speaking of the devil, heave comes the doctor right now," she said.

"Good, because I'm ready to get the fuck up out of here," Money said. After signing a few discharge papers, Money was good to go. Money and Young Money got in the car with each other.

"Wassup, nigga, you aight? Let me find out niggas thought they was gon' die," Young Money said as he lit up the back wood filled with the best of cookies. He inhaled the smoke and then released it through his nose. He passed the wood to Money. As he inhaled the cookie smoke, he damn near choked. As he was coughing, he gave the wood back to Young Money.

"Da fuck you put in that shit?" Money said.

"Oh, that's that new beeswax they got at the club that shit dope high."

"Fuck yea, that shit almost killed a nigga." After they passed the wood back and forth, they both were feeling the effect of the cookies. As they parked in the cut, they got down to the basics. "So look, bra, I think I know who shot me. I seen they face a lil bit."

"Who the fuck was it? I'ma smack one of dem niggas. Was it them G-block niggas?"

"Nah, it can't be them. Them niggas pussy. Had to been them harbor niggas. They be acting like they want smoke."

"Nigga, if you shut tha fuck up in let me tell you," Money said.

"Aight, since you know it all, I think that was a hit. I seen a Chinese-looking nigga, bra. I think it got something to do with Mulan in them licks she been putting us on with."

"You think so?" Young Money said.

"I mean, it's only one way to find out."

Mulan was out baby shopping with Fendi and Chanele. "Girl, this gonna look cute on lil Money," Fendi said.

"Un huh, don't start that shit, Fendi. His name ain't gon' be nothing with no Young or no Money," Mulan said. "And how y'all know he ain't gon' be no she?"

"And when is you 'pose to find out what you having?" replied Chanele.

"I want to do a gender reveal," said Mulan.

"Oh yea, that's gone be nice. Can I help you plan it? You know I'm good at doing that type of stuff," said Fendi.

"Since you so good at it, why you ain't had no baby yet?" Mulan said.

"Girl, don't trip. You knew I'ma have one when I'm ready."

"Okay, I hear you, and wassup with you, Chanele? You've been acting mighty quiet," Mulan said.

"I'm just thinking about Money. I hope he all right. I been worried about him."

"Girl, he gon' be all right. The doctor said it was a flesh wound. The bullet went in and out," Mulan replied.

"Why you don't just call da nigga and see what he doing? He probley wit another bitch," Fendi said.

"Why you gotta be so negative, Fendi?" said Chanele.

"Y'all need to stop."

"Nah, this bitch always on some other shit."

"You in yo feeling over this nigga. Let me find out, Chanele, this nigga got you open."

Chanele was done talking because she knew deep down she was falling for Money, and she couldn't help it. Mulan was done shopping for the baby; she was ready to go home.

"Y'all ready to go? I'm tired."

"Yeah, let's get up out of here," Fendi said.

Once Mulan made it home, she saw an envelope on her doormat. When she opened it, she saw something that made her heart drop. It was a note from her uncle. It was stamped in red ink with one Asian word, but it described many words. Mulan opened up her door as she got inside. She searched every room door in the closet. After she finished, she dialed Young Money. Ring, ring. "Wassup, babe? What you doing?" Young Money said. Mulan couldn't hold back her tears; she couldn't even get no words out. All she could do was cry. "Baby, don't worry. I'm fenna be on my way. Where you at?"

"I'm at home," she said.

"Aight, I'm on my way." Young Money hung up the phone and headed to Mulan's house. He was driving like a bat out of hell tryna get to Mulan. Once he made it to her house, he ran up the stairs, almost tripping over himself from moving so fast. As he got in the house, Mulan ran to him. "It's gon' be aight. Whoever did this to you, they dead, you hear me. I'ma make sure of it," Young Money said. Mulan handed Young Money the envelope. "What is this?"

"Open it. It's from my uncle. I think he had something to do with Money getting shot," she said as she began crying again.

"Don't cry, babe. It's not your fault. We knew what time it was when shit got real, so don't stress yourself. But look, this what I want you to do. I want you to pack some clothes and go to Fendi house. Call me when you get there, okay."

Mulan nodded her head up and down. "Young Money, I love you."

"I love you too."

"I'ma bout to go take care of some shit."

"Please be careful. I don't know what I would do if something was to happen to you," Mulan said.

"Don't trip, babe. Everything gon' be good. Just pack yo shit, and we gon' talk more after I finish taking care of business." After he gave Mulan a kiss on her lips, he gave her a kiss on her stomach.

Young Money had his mind on murder. *These fucking China boys got me fucked up. First they come through my projects, almost killed my brother, then they sending notes to my bitch house. I got something for these bitches.*

Ring, ring. Young Money was broke out his chain of thoughts when he heard his phone ringing. "Wassup, bra, everything good?" Money said.

"Nah, but look, that shit you was telling me about the China boy that was Mulan people, but look, I'm fenna pull up on you. We gotta figure some shit out."

Once Young Money got back to the city, he went to go holla at Pedro that was his plug. Ring, ring. "Wassup, buddy? What you been up too?"

"Man, Pedro, it's been a lot of shit going on. We need to talk. Is you at the shop?"

"Yeah, I'm here. Come stop by."

"Aight, I'm on my way." After Young Money got off the phone with Pedro, he went to go get Money. Ring, ring. "Come outside, bra."

"Aight."

Money came walking down the stairs. He had a lil pain from the gunshot wound, but other than that, he was good. "So wassup? What's the play?" Money said to Young Money as he got in the car.

"Man, bra, this shit crazy. First thing first, we gotta move Moms out the way. That shit that happened wit you was a close call. You almost lost yo life, my nigga," Young Money said.

"I'm already knowing, bra, we deffinitely gotta move smarter."

"A lot of shit been crazy niggas been getting to they bag life good. We young niggas gettin money, and we got bitches."

"Ayy, look though, we definitely on dem China boys," Money said.

"You already know Mulan gon' give us the drop, and we gonna do are shit. I'm fenna pull up on Pedro right now and see wassup wit dem fullies," Young Money told Money."

As they pulled up to Pedro's store, Young Money and Money got out the car and rang the bell to get in. Ring, ring. "Wassup, buddy? Ayy, P, I'm outside," Young Money said. *Bzzzzz*. Pedro had let Young Money and Money in.

"Wassup with my boy? How can I help you?"

"Man, P, I needs some heavy artillery. I'm fenna start a war."

"Hah hah, I war hugh, I got just the thing to get the job done. Follow me." They had followed Pedro into his gun room. When Young Money and Money saw all the guns on the wall, they felt like they died and went to heaven.

"Okay, that's what the fuck I'm talking about. This shit right here gon' fuck some shit up," Money said as he grabbed a Carbon 15. He was in awe from the beauty of the gun.

"So look, Pedro, I need a few handguns, and I need some shops. How much you're gonna charge me?" Young Money said.

"Okay, my friend, I'll give you ten handguns and ten machine guns for 50,000."

"Come on, Pedro. You kind of high on them prices," Money said.

"These are state-of-the-art guns, everything brand-new. I tell you what, I'll throw in some silencers. How about that?"

"Now you talking my language, Pedro. You know I fuck wit dem silencers," Young Money said.

"So do we have a deal?" said Pedro.

Young Money looked at Money, and they both nodded they head. "It's good. We a take it." Young Money gave Pedro the money.

"Hey, YM, let me holla at you real quick," Pedro said.

"Wassup, P? What's the deal?"

"Ayy, not to be in your business, but is everything aight? You ain't never purchased these many guns at one time."

"You know what's funny?" Young Money said.

"And what's that?" Pedro replied.

"People always say I'm not tryna be in yo business, but the whole time trying to figure out what's going on not to be rude, P, but I got some shit going on. But as you can see, I'ma handle it," Young Money said.

"Okay, my friend. Can I help you with anything else?"

"Nah, I'm good for now, Pedro, but I'ma get at you. I'ma have some more gold for you soon."

"That's what I like to hear. I like to make money, Young Money, so make sure when you take care of business, you focus on getting the Denaro. It's all about the Denaro," Pedro said.

"Aight, P, I'ma get at you in a minute," Young Money stated. As they grabbed the guns, Young Money and Money got in the car.

"So what's the play?" Money said.

"We fenna go drop these cannons off at the trap, then I'm fenna go pull up on Mulan and holla at her about these China boys. And where sis at?"

"She at Chanele house."

When Money heard Chanele's name, a smile came to his face. "That's crazy. My nigga straight thirsty," Young Money said.

"Fuck, what you talking 'bout? I ain't had no pussy since I got shot, so you know I'm on my horn dog shit." Young Money couldn't do nothing but laugh. Once they dropped the guns off, they slid to town. As they got in front of Chanele's house, Young Money called Mulan. Ring, ring.

"Hello," Mulan said.

"Ayy, babe, open the front door. I'm outside."

"Aight, here I come." Once Mulan opened the door, they went inside. Young Money went to go sit on the couch where Mulan was sleeping for the night. Money had went straight to the refrigerator; he was looking for something to eat. As he was going through the refrigerator, Chanele had walked in the living room.

"Uggh, un boy, what is you doing all in my refrigerator?"

"Oh, yo fridgerator? So where the food at because a nigga starving," Money said.

"At yo house," she said wit a lil attitude.

"Well, excuse me, my bad. Y'all must ain't got y'all food stamps."

"Boy, ain't nobody on no warefare. We got jobs over here, unlike them bumb bitches you be fucking wit."

"I see you got jokes, but fareal can you make something to eat?"

"Yeah, Chanele, make something to eat," Mulan said with a grin on her face. She knew Chanele didn't feel like cooking.

"Bitch, you get on my nerves," Chanele said to Mulan.

"I love you too, cuz," Mulan replied back. As Chanele went to the deep freezer to go grab some steak and prawns, Fendi came walking out in her T-shirt and panties. Her ass was all out. Mulan had whispered to Young

Money, "You bet not." Young Money had that "what you talking about" look on his face. Money couldn't do nothing but stare. He definitely was enjoying the view. Chanele had to clear her throat just to break his stare. "Damn, Fendi, you ain't gon' put no clothes on," Mulan said.

"Bitch, this is my house, and ain't nobody trippin' off of Money and Young Money. They ain't no boddy. And what you cooking, sis?"

"Some steak, baked potatos, and shrimp."

"Okay, bitch, I see you cooking for yo nigga, but a bitch didn't want to cook earlier," Fendi said.

"Right," Mulan chipped in. "All of a sudden, Money over here, bitches ready to cook."

"Don't come for me, Mulan," Chanele said. "I'm not in the mood. And the only reason why I'm cooking is for my little cuzn inside your stomach, so y'all lucky I'm cooking."

When Chanele mentioned this, Young Money saw his train of thought come back to him. "Ayy, babe, let me holla at you real quick." Mulan led Young Money to the back patio.

"Wassup, babe, what's on yo mind?" Mulan said.

As Young Money wrapped his arms around her stomach, holding her from the back, he took a deep breath. "Man, babe, shit been crazy these past few weeks. I know I been in these streets taking care of business, but I feel like we ain't been able to be together how we usually do. And I want you to know once I get to the bottom of this shit, it's gon' be about you and the baby."

"I hear you, babe. I already know." Mulan was getting turned on by Young Money's touching. Her pussy was getting wet. She knew shit was real, but her hormones were going through the roof.

Mulan let out a soft moan; just his touch had her ready. "So look, babe, what's the deal wit yo folks? They got me fucked up. They shot my brother, then they threatening you. Them muthafuckas got me fucked up I'm ready to kill all them bitches."

"I know, babe. I'm wit you. I'm on yo side, and I think that was my cuzn kid that's my uncle youngest son. He be longing with the triads and Chinatown. He hang out at a tea shop inside Chinatown."

"Okay, look, tomorrow I need you to show me where the spot is." Mulan nodded her head. "Don't trip, babe. We gon' be good, and we also need to find a new spot somewhere under." Mulan was so submissive when it came to Young Money she was ready for whatever. He looked at her in her face.

"Do you trust me?"

"Of course I trust you. The question is do you trust me."

"You know I trust you. You mean the world to me. You and my seed is my world." After he said that, he gave her a kiss, and they headed back in.

"Damn, what? Y'all got lost outside?" Fendi said as Young Money and Mulan came back in.

"Mind yo business, Ms. Nosey," Mulan said. "And is the food done? Me and my baby are hungry."

"You know what? Y'all hella greedy, and y'all didn't even help me, but its good. I still did my thing," Chanele said. After making the plates, everybody ate their food.

The next day, Young Money and Money were in traffic. Mulan showed them where the kid be hanging at so they were ready to put they murder game down, dressed in all black. They both had on ski mask that covered the whole face. After looking they target in, they was ready to do they shit. Money had a Drako, and Young Money had a mini M-16 with a silencer on it. As they bent the corner, they let off bullets at a rapid speed. Flop flop flop flop flop . . . Bow bow Bow bow . . . Boom boom boom. Somebody tried to get back off at Young Money, but as he maneuvered the M-16 around, he hit his target right in the head. Money saw kid's crawling for dear life. "Where the fuck you think you going?" Money said after he kicked him in the side.

"You know who you're fucking wit? My dad is the leader of the triads."

"Bitch, you think I give a fuck about that?" Money said, then let the whole clip off in him.

"Come on, bra. We up out of here. The police on they way," Young Money said.

Once they got in the car, they slid off nice and easy. "That's what the fuck I'm talking 'bout. I got dat nigga. He was tryna crawl under a table and hide. I fead that nigga wit the whole clip," Money said as Young Money was getting on the freeway. He saw several SFPD rushing to the scene. He had a big grin on his face. He just got away wit murder literally.

"You seen all them cop cars? Shit hot right now. We gotta go duck off. Shit fenna get real wit these China boys. We gotta be on are shit. We just killed a member from the triads, and from what Mulan was telling me, them muthafuckas wit the bullshit," Young Money said. "That China boy you got on, that was the head of the triad mob son, so you know we gotta move extra mean," Young Money said.

"Aint Jay still at getting them packs off?" Money replied.

"Yeah, he should be on his way out here tonight. Dude been MIA. We need him out here."

"We do, but we also need him in New York so we can move them PS, but you said he ran through them bitches."

"Yeah, he got all of 'em off. It was like 1,000 PS, so you know we got a nice bag coming," Young Money said.

"But look, bra, we gotta find Moms somewhere else to live. It's about time we get her a house," Money said.

"Bra, you know Moms ain't gon' want to move. She been staying in the hood our whole life. You know that apartment building the only thing she got of Dad," Young Money replied. "But we can go look at some spots in Sacramento. They got some phat spots out there."

"We should go do that now. We ain't got shit else to do. We can just cash out for a five bedroom," Money said.

"Yeah, that sounds cool, but how?"

"We just gon' cash out, and we gon' have to show a paper trail to where it shows where the money coming from," said Young Money.

"You know what we can do? We can have Mulan sign for the house. She got a salary that makes over a 100K. So we can just have her put the house in her name. Matter of fact, let me call her real quick. Ring, ring. Mulan picked up on the first ring.

"Oh my god, babe, is everything all right? I was watching the news, and . . . and I thought . . ." Mulan couldn't hold back her tears.

"Everything gon' be aight. I'm good, babe, so stop crying." Mulan was holding back her tears; she knew what she signed up for. "Look, babe, I need you to do me a favor. I need you to go to my mom house. Once you get there, I want you to go to my room and get some money out my safe. You still remember the combination code to the safe."

"Yes, babe, I remember."

"Aight, grab like $100,000 and meet me in Sac."

"Okay, I love you."

"I love you too," Young Money said. "Aight, everything good," he said to Money after he hung up wit Mulan. "Wassup, nigga, roll up you over there textn'? Put them fingers to use," Young Money said, giving Money the cookies to roll up. As Money was rolling up the wood, he was playing out the drill he had earlier. "What you over there smiling about?"

"I was just thinking . . ." Money had lit the wood and inhaled the cookie smoke. "I was just thinking how we creeped on them bing-bings and did are shit."

Young Money had to crack a smile because he knew did they shit, and there wasn't no witnesses. "I know," Young Money said. "That shit felt good. We fenna get to this bag. We just started a war wit these China boys." Money hit the wood one more time and passed it to Young Money. As he inhaled the cookie smoke, he pulled up to the realtor's place to go see if he could find a house for his mom. When they walked in the real estate office, Young Money and Money were smelling like a pound of weed.

"Hi, how can I help you?" the clerk said.

"I'm tryna buy a house, and I have cash," Young Money said.

That was music to the sales clerk's ear. She knew by locking in this sale, she was gon' get a big comision. "Okay, well, I'm going to refer you to one of our realtors, and she can help you." Once the clerk phoned for the realtor, Young Money's phone rung.

"Wassup, babe? I'm here. Where y'all at?" Mulan said.

"We in the main office."

"All right, I'm fenna park, and I be right in."

"Hi, how can I help you today?" the real estate lady said.

"Um, I'm tryna buy a house, somewhere nice and quiet for me and my family. My girl on her way in. You can talk to her about the money and legal stuff," Young Money said.

"Okay, will do," said the real estate lady. Mulan came walking in. "So you are the lady we've been waiting for?" the real estate lady said. "Let's get down to business. Well, for starters, we have several new houses we just built in the Sacramento Hills. The view is lovely. I can take you to the area if you like, or I can show you over the tablet."

"Uhm, it don't matter." She looked at Young Money for confirmation. He nodded his head.

"Okay, well, let's get started. This house right here is a four-bedroom three-bathroom modern-style house. It has a nice view. It's a school nearby for the little one." She looked at Mulan; her stomach was getting big. "And we have a five-bedroom four-bathroom with a swimming pool in the backyard for the price of $550,000. You can put a down payment of $10,000, and your mortgage will be based on your credit rate, so if you can give me your social and your first and last name, I can run your credit score." Mulan gave the lady the information she needed. "Okay, you've been approved. Your credit score was a 790, so your mortgage will only be $2,000 a month. So do you like the five-bedroom more again?"

She looked at Young Money for confirmation. "We would take it," Young Money said. As he was ready to go, he told Mulan to sign the papers, and he was gone to meet up with her later, and he told her to spend the rest of the money to furnish the house.

Young Money and Money got back in the car. They had to go get Jay from the airport. Once they got to SF Airport, Jay was waiting outside. "Wassup wit you, niggas?" Jay said. "I been waiting here for hella long." Young Money broke out laughing. They was high off the cookies; they just had finished smoking.

"Man, bra, today been a long day. We had hella shit going on one, and Money slid on dem China boys. We did are shit," Young Money said.

"Okay, niggas got they feet wet," Jay replied.

"Yeah, you know them bing bings thought they was fucking wit some rookies, Money said.

"But wassup with that bag? What the count looking like?" Young Money said.

"Oh, the count looking good. I slid through customs wit the duffle bag."

"So where we fenna count up at?" Jay said.

"We gon' have to go to a telly or something," Money replied. "Shit been hot in the hood. We just copped Moms a house in Sac. I got Mulan signing for the papers. Right now, we should be able to move in. In a few days," Young Money said.

"Man, fuck all that telly shit. Let's go to my spot."

"Jay, you know moms be tripping. That ain't fenna happen," Money said.

"You niggas hella funny. I don't even stay with my parents no more. I moved in wit Fendi."

"Say it ain't so. You feeling o girl like that, I mean, that's wassup, though, but I think she a lil fast for you," Young Money said.

"Yeah, I hear you. I know what I'm doing," Jay said. Once they pulled up to Fendi's house, they got out the car.

"Ayy, Jay, let me find out Fendi got you pussy wooped," Money said. Jay had to laugh that one-off. As he put the key in the door, he thought to himself, *I ain't gon' lie. Even though Fendi got some rachet ways, she still got some good-ass pussy, and she hella cool. Fuck what these niggas talking about?*

"Earth to Jay. Open the door, nigga. Where you went to? Lah Lah Land? This nigga over here siked out daydreaming and shit," Money said.

"Fuck you, nigga. I was thinking about he was saying . . ." As he was opening the door, his words got cut short when he saw Fendi standing in the doorway wit her hand on her hip.

"What y'all think y'all doing? This is not the trap house on Oakdale."

Young Money and Money looked at Jay to say something. "Babe, chill out. We fenna count up real quick, and we gon' cut in a minute."

"We ain't going nowhere. I haven't been with you and a whole week, so you're staying home, and I need some dick," she said, then gave him a kiss and went back to her room. Chanele was on the couch watching a rerun of *Love & Hip Hop*. Jay set the duffle bag on the table and looked at Chanele.

"Boy, what is you looking? I'm not moving, so whatever y'all gotta do, y'all mine as well do it because I'm watching my show."

"My nigga, that's a rerun anyway," Money said.

"It don't matter. This is my house, my couch, and my TV."

"Aight, that shit y'all got going on y'all mind as well fuck and get it over with. It's obvious y'all both like each other." Young Money said.

"Nah, he like Mi-Mi."

"Says who?" Money said. "If you really wanna know. I like you."

Chanele didn't know Money was serious or playing, so she said, "Yea, whatever. We a see." Money chuckled.

Jay had dumped the money on the coffee table. "Okay, that's what I'm talking about. Let's count his money," Young Money said. Chanele couldn't believe her eyes. She ain't never seen that much money in her life; she knew they was getting money, but she didn't know it was on that level. Young Money grabbed some stacks and started counting. Money was counting his stacks as well.

Fendi came walking, and when she seen all that money on the table, "Oow, who money is that?"

"Not yours," Money said in a joking matter.

"Boy, best believe whatever Jay cut is is mines, so yeah."

"Okay, hold up. This ain't got nothing to do with me," Jay said.

"Jay, you know wassup," Fendi said and walked to the kitchen.

"So, Money, when you gon' stop playing with my sister? You know she feeling you."

"Why is you lying? Fendi, ain't nobody worried about that boy," Chanele said.

"Man, ain't nobody playing. She be on some other shi.t I be tryna fuck with her," Money replied.

"Ain't nobody got time for yo games, Money. You be having too much going on, and if you think you fenna be having me look stupid in these streets, you got another thing coming," said Chanele.

"Oh shit, this shit better then *Love & Hip Hop*," Young Money said.

"Shut, shut up, lil messy. You ain't slick either. My cuzin told me about that lil bitch TaTa," Fendi said.

"I don't know what you talking about," said Young Money, laughing it off.

"Yeah, I bet, but tell that lil girl when she tried to come for my cuzin, she came for me too, so just know we on that bitch when my cuz drop," replied Fendi.

"Man, you trippin, my nigga, but when I find out who she is, I'ma let you know."

"Ayy, Jay how much you counted up?" Young Money said.

"Shit like 125,000," he said, smiling.

"What about you, Money?"

"The same," Money replied.

"Okay, that's wassup. That's $375,000 in total, so we get 125 apiece. Not bad for the first flip," Young Money said.

Chanele was looking as they put the stacks of money in rubber bands. Mulan came walking in the house as Young Money put the rest of the money back in the duffle bag. "Wassup, babe? How did everything go?"

"It went good. I got the house, I put the down payment down, and the furniture is paid for. They said it should be delivered by tomorrow."

"That's wassup. We gon' surprise Moms tomorrow, and her b-day coming up. That's right on time," Young Money said.

"Wassup, cuz, you look a lil tired," Chanele said.

"I'm fine. I just been cramping. This baby been acting up. I'm fenna go lay down in your room," Mulan said. As Mulan went back to the room, Young Money followed behind her.

"Babe, you aight?"

"Yeah, I'm good. It's just been a long day, and I just need to lay down."

"I know shit been crazy for the past few days, but its gon' be good, I promise you. I just need you to be on yo shit. If something happen to you and my seed. I don't know what I would do."

"Don't think like that, baby. I need you to stay focused in these streets, especially going to war with my family. They're going to try in come for you," Mulan said.

"Listen, babe, my gun bust just like there's I'ma kill each and every one of dem bitches."

"Come here," Mulan said as she grabbed his hand and put it on her stomach. He felt the baby move; seeing that brought a smile to his face. As he reached over to give Mulan a kiss, she grabbed him closer, and they began to kiss passionately. As their tongues touched, all the stress and worries left Mulan's body. She let out soft moans as he kissed her stomach. Mulan's love box was throbbing and begging for attention. She couldn't take it no more. She got up and led Young Money to the bathroom.

"Where we going?"

"To the bathroom. I'm not fenna fuck you in my cousin bead. That is triflin'."

"We could have put a sheet down," Young Money said, laughing it off.

"No, you is crazy." Once they got in the bathroom, Mulan turned the shower on and started taking Young Money's clothes off. Once they were both naked, they got in the shower. Mulan let the warm water run down her body. Young Money started kissing Mulan slow and deep.

"You know I love you," he said.

"How much?" she said between kisses.

"I love you more than a fat kid love cakes. You know my style. I say anything to make you smile. You so crazy."

As Young Money pinned Mulan to the wall, he had her legs spread open on the shower railings. As he went down on her, he found her clitoris and started kissing and licking it. "Oooww, Young Money, that feel so good. Fuck, I love you," she said as she grabbed his head for leverage. Young Money continued to eat Mulan's pussy as she came back to back. "Damn, babe, you gon' make me pass out."

"I'm not done with you yet," he said.

"Oh really? Well, I'm not done with you either." As she stroked his already rock-hard penis, she bent over and guided his dick inside her. As he inserted her wet pussy, Mulan began moaning again. "Unn huh, yes, babe, give me that dick."

"Fuck, babe, this pussy so good."

As Mulan threw her ass back on Young Money, she felt her orgasm coming. "Oh my god, baby. I'm cumming. I'ma bout to cum," she screamed to the high heavens.

As she was coming, Young Money busted a fat nut inside her. "Fuck, wooo shit, that was just everything," Young Money said as he slid out of Mulan. Once they finished rinsing off, Mulan had some new boxer breifs and socks for Young Money to put on. As they got dressed, they headed back to the living room. Mulan was walking to the couch. She felt a sharp pain in her stomach, then she felt something come down her leg. "Babe, you aight?" Young Money ran to her side.

"I think my water broke. Call the ambulances."

Chanele called 911. "Hello, this is 911. What's your emergency?"

"My cousin water broke, and we need a ambulance."

"Okay, ma'am, someone will be there shortly."

Mulan was taking deep breaths, and the only thing that was on her mind was her unborn child. She did not want to lose her child. "Babe, everything gon' be aight. The ambulances is on their way. Just stay calm," Young Money said. He was a lil shook. His first seed life was in jeopardy. He knew Mulan wasn't due until a couple of months. Once the ambulance got there, they put Mulan on the gurney and took her away. "Fuck, bra, this shit crazy. How the fuck this shit happening right now?" Young Money was yelling out loud.

"We can't panic. We gotta be strong for Mulan," Chanele said.

Fendi came running out of her room. "What happened was I was asleep, and I heard sirens. Oh my god, where is Mulan?"

"We gotta get to the hospital," Young Money said.

Once everybody got ready to leave, some got into seperate cars. As they got to the hospital, Young Money went to the desk clerk. "Hi, I'm looking for Mulan Jones."

"One moment. Okay, she's on the fourth floor." Young Money and everybody else hurriedly got on the elevator.

Once they got to the fourth floor, they were greeted by the doctor of the hour. "Hi, I'm Dr. Bentley. I take it you're looking for Mulan Jones. She heavily sedated. The lil girl almost didn't make, but we did everything we could and saved her. She's a lil soldier. She was born premature, five pounds, six ounces." Hearing that brought tears to Young Money's eyes. He was happy and hurting at the same time.

"Can we see the baby?" Fendi said.

"Since we just finished doing surgery on the mother, I guess some of you can come to the back. Just two at a time."

Young Money and Fendi went first. "Oh my god, she is so beautiful," Fendi said. "Why she so small? Is she gon' get bigger?" Young Money said.

"Yes, she will," said the nurse who was watching over her.

"Everything gon' be all right, my lil princess, I promise you." After everybody saw the baby, they went to stop by to check on Mulan. She was heavy sedated due to the surgery. "Hey, babe, I love you. I hope you can hear me. The baby made it. Are lil princess made it," he said as he grabbed her hand. If only Young Money knew that Mulan heard every word.

"I love you too, Young Money," she said to herself. As they began to leave, Young Money gave Mulan a kiss on the lips and left.

The receptionist was doing some last-minute paperwork. As she looked up, she thought she was seeing doubles, but she wasn't. What she was seeing was Mulan's cuzin Ling Ling. She was a split image of Mulan. "HI, how can I help you?"

"I'm looking for Mulan Lee?"

"Um, we don't have anybody under that name."

"Excuse me, it's Mulan Jones."

"Okay, I found her, but it's past visiting hours. Who might you be?" the receptionist said.

"I'm her cousin."

"Okay, you guys look just alike. I tell you what, I'll give you a few minutes to see the baby, and Ms. Jones is still sedated, so she's sleep." Ling Ling went to go see the baby first. When she walked in the room, she saw the baby hooked up to tubes and a breathing machine.

"My little butterfly," she said in her native tongue. "You are so precious. I'm going to love you forever." As she was fenna leave, she stopped by Mulan's room. "Hey, lil cuz, long time no see. I really thought everything that was happening was the opisitions, but no, it was you this whole time, you in your lil black boyfriend causing all these problems. And my brother was killed by his brother. I'm not gon' lie, I do want some chocolate. I might fuck his brother," she said, whispering in her ear. Mulan could hear her, but she couldn't say nothing due to her being sedated. Ling Ling gave Mulan a kiss on her forehead; you would have thought it was a kiss of death. She then left out.

The next day, Mulan woke up from a dreamlike state. She had remembered bits and pieces of what happened prior to her being at the hospital. The nurse had came back in. "Hello, Ms. Jones, I see you finally woke up. You must be thirsty," the nurse said as she poured her something to drink. Once Mulan quenched her thirst, she instantly asked about her baby. "Where's my baby?"

"Oh, let me go get her," the nurse said.

"It's a her?" Mulan said.

"Yeah, she was born premature, but she made it. Let me go get her for you." When the nurse came back, she was empty-handed.

"Um, excuse me, ma'am, where's my baby?" The nurse couldn't answer. "Where the fuck is my baby?" Mulan started kicking and screaming.

"Please, ma'am, calm down. We are having some difficulties locating her."

"So you mean to fucking tell me that you lost my baby?"

"Technically, we think somebody took her. We have some footage of the last person who came to see you. Do you want to see it?"

"Yes, please, can you show it to me?" The nurse had the laptop and showed her the footage. What she saw made her heart drop. It was her cuzzin Ling Ling taking her baby. "This bitch," she said out loud.

"Ma'am, do you know her? If you do, we need you to make a police report." Mulan couldn't take it no more. She started kicking and screaming. "Ma'am, you have to calm down." The nurse called the doctors in, and they gave her a shot to calm her down to put her to sleep.

The end

Index

Lightning Source UK Ltd.
Milton Keynes UK
UKHW041846190321
380669UK00008B/401/J

9 781664 161979